Chapter One

I'd always loved airports. Checking in and stepping into the departures lounge made me feel important. But today was special. Today I was getting an international flight.

As I made my way towards the international departures lounge with my big ticket in my hand and my airline bag over my shoulder I tried to look nonchalant. People-watchers will be checking me out, I said to myself. Wondering if I am somebody. Waiting for my plane was a pain. Many people were eating, but a brief look along the buffet's servery failed to arouse my appetite. I had a newspaper, but after gazing at the front page for several minutes without reading a word, I stuffed it back into my bag. Then, at long last, the public address system told me that my flight was now boarding.

As I stepped aboard the plane a smiling stewardess asked to see my pass. She told me I was at the back on the right. I wondered if her not showing me to my seat had anything to do with me. I turned away. The plane seemed already full. And, lots of people were still moving about, taking off jackets and coats and stuffing things into the overhead storage lockers. No wonder the stewardess stayed put, I said to myself. I squeezed and excused my way down the aisle. This got me slightly flustered but I was delighted to find that I had a window seat. Despite my being a nervy passenger I enjoyed looking down at the world during a flight.

In no time everything was trembling slightly. The engines were running. We would soon be on our way. By this time a large bloke, with black-rimmed glasses and black greasy hair, had settled down in the seat next to me. I didn't say anything. I always tried to keep myself to myself when I was travelling.

As the plane slid back and away from its gate I caught sight of a woman waving towards the plane from one of the terminal's windows. Before I knew it my hand was up and waving back.

'Girlfriend?'

'Well, er,' I said.

'That's the worst part. Leaving the loved ones behind,' said my neighbour.

'Oh, most certainly,' I said, wondering how long it had been since I'd seen my mum or my dad or my sister or any of my friends.

'George. George Ellis,' said the big man.

I shook the large hand that had been pushed towards me. 'Jack,' I said, 'I'm Jack. Pleased to meet you, George.'

'Where are you heading for, Jack?'

I felt like saying something facetious about the fact that the flight destination was Amsterdam, but I managed to control myself. 'Amsterdam,' I said.

'Initially, that is. Then onto Kuwait.' George's face lit up.
'Ha!' exclaimed George. I seemed to know what was coming next. 'Me too,' he added. I was right. 'I've got a job at the College of Commerce. I convinced them I could teach computing. How about you, Jack?'
'Me too,' I said. 'Well, not exactly, I'll be teaching English.'
'What a coincidence,' said George, 'our getting seats together. Well, maybe not. The agency probably asked for adjacent seats for us.'
It turned out that George and I had much in common. He was divorced and I had just recently been dumped by my girlfriend. He had lost both his parents in a road accident when he was in his teens, and had no brothers or sisters. I still had my family and friends at home but I had moved to London and had spent the past few months job-hunting in Chiswick. Both of us had been unemployed for quite a while, living rather solitary lives. And, at thirty-five George was just one year older than I.
While we were getting away from the terminal and into the air I watched our progress through my window. But something made me turn and look towards George. There was nothing I wanted to say, which was just as well. George was fast asleep.
On hearing that we had begun our descent into Schipol I gave George a nudge. He looked right and

left and yawned and stretched before thanking me for waking him.

At Schipol, George stated that he badly needed a fix of caffeine, and within a few minutes of our entering the terminal building his nose had led us to a small coffee bar. We sat on high stools. George didn't speak while he was drinking his coffee. He seemed to be thinking about and judging every sip. Then, as he placed his empty cup on the saucer on the bar he let out a loud, 'Ah! That's better.' I wondered how George would cope with there being no booze in Kuwait. He explained that since he was almost teetotal he would have no problem with that. I confessed to having my doubts since I enjoyed an occasional single malt and a pint of real ale.

'Well, you won't have much choice,' George laughed. 'Unless of course you are willing to pay about sixty pounds for a bottle on the black market. Apparently, that's the going rate out there, so, you'd better start getting used to the idea that there ain't going to be no beer for a year.'

'If it gets too bad I can always come home,' I said.

'Now, that might not be quite so easy,' said George, replacing the smile on his face with a serious look. 'Until your contract is up, that is.'

'What do you mean?' I asked.

'Well, it's obviously not an easy country to get into, mate. And I reckon getting out could be just as difficult. What do you think those twelve passport photographs are all about? A great big bureaucratic machine, mate. Lots and lots of red tape.'

'I hadn't thought of that.'

The flight to Kuwait was just four and a half hours but it felt more like four and a half days. But, it was no time at all to George. He slept the whole way. The pilot's announcement that we were approaching Kuwait was like a piece of my favourite music to my ears. Just a few minutes later, the pilot announced that Kuwait City was now visible on the left side. I gazed out into the darkness but could see nothing. But then, as the plane banked steeply to the left, Kuwait City came into view. A large, sparkling, white diamond on a jet-black backcloth. Not quite the quaint little place one might have expected, I thought. Of course, I said to myself, lots of oil, lots of power stations, lots of electricity, lots of lights. I suddenly realised I knew little about what I was getting myself into.

Only a dozen or so passengers got off at Kuwait. While we were marching along the arrivals route George said that he would rather have been going all the way to Dubai. He said that by all accounts it was a great place. I mentioned my hearing that you could get a pint there.

As we approached the immigration barrier we slowed and eventually stopped. There were three quite separate queues waiting to go through.

'Which one do you reckon we should tag onto, then, George?' George pulled on a pensive face and, gently stroking his chin, looked at each of the queues in turn.

'The queue on the left is all guys in traditional Arab gear. There are lots of different styles of dress in the middle queue, everybody has dark hair and I see no white faces. Hmm. Now, this queue on the right. It comprises guys in either a suit or jazzy shirt and casual trousers. And all are amazingly white skinned. So, I think the percentage move here would be to join the pale faces.'

'Right,' I said. What a pillock, I thought. Why wasn't I able to suss out the queues like that? It was so obvious.

A fair-haired, lightly tanned bloke wearing a light tan jacket and trousers came towards us. 'Jack and George?' he asked. George and I said, yes, in unison. He introduced himself as Nigel and said he was the Director of Studies at the College. He offered his hand to George and said, 'George, I presume.' George simply nodded and shook the man's hand. Our welcomer then turned to me. 'And you must be Jack.'

'That's me,' I replied. I wondered how Nigel could have been so apparently sure as to which one of us was George. He asked us for our papers. He then asked us to excuse him for a few minutes and strode off.

There were lots of people milling about, including sub-machinegun-toting policemen. I had seen armed policemen on television many times, but having one pass just a few feet away sent a shiver down my spine. It was scary. I thought about how I ought to behave in order to look inoffensive. I decided to try to look sheepish. What do you do to look sheepish? I asked myself.

Nigel returned. He looked towards George.

'Blithering idiot' he said. George's eyebrows shot up. 'Oh, I do apologise, George. Not your good self. No, I was referring to that horrible little immigration chap. Rubber-stamping a few sheets of paper seemed to stretch his intellectual capacity to the limit. Right, gentlemen, I shall meet with you again on the other side by the luggage pick-up point.'

'Bye', George and I said together.

It took about an hour to get through immigration. Nigel had sussed out our cases and was standing between them. 'Right, gentlemen, if you would care to follow me I have a cab waiting.' He turned and stepped out towards the terminal exit like a man in a hurry. George and I followed on in his slipstream, doing our best to keep up. The taxi was a large American car. While the driver was stashing our cases into the boot, George and I clambered into the back seat. Nigel said something to the driver in

Arabic, and off we went. In no time, we were on a brightly lit motorway, and travelling far too quickly for my liking. I felt better when we joined another motorway where there was heavy, stopping-and-starting traffic. Nigel turned and said we were nearing Kuwait City and that the traffic was almost always like this at this point. Before long, we turned off the motorway and into shadowy side streets. Just a few minutes later, we pulled up outside a tall building with a low wall around it. I counted six storeys. Nigel swung round. 'Here we are then,' he said gleefully. I knew I would be living in a flat, but I had envisaged some sort of four-in-a-block arrangement. It hadn't even occurred to me that there might be tall buildings in Kuwait. Nigel said that our flat was on the top floor. George immediately stated that he was not a happy man. He said that he had been led to believe that he would have his own flat. I clearly remember being told by the bloke who interviewed me that new teachers would have to share for a while, but I decided to keep my mouth shut about this. I reasoned that George would not appreciate my mentioning this at this point. Nigel managed to pacify George a little by saying that his sharing was just a temporary measure and that he would get him his own flat as soon as possible.

In the ground floor of the block there were the start of the stairs, which were marble, a lift and one door, which Nigel described as the caretaker's caboose. Nigel added that the caretaker is known as the *harres*. George complained about our being on the top floor. Nigel assured us that the lift was well maintained and very reliable. The door of the flat opened directly into the living room. This was a huge room, which had a full-width window at one end. Directly opposite the door a wide hall gave access to two bedrooms, a bathroom and a kitchen. Nigel pointed out that the kitchen was fully equipped and that he had stocked up the fridge.

Nigel's face lit up. 'Okay,' he said, 'I'd better give you some money.' He gave us two hundred dinars each and advised us to try to quickly get used to the fact that each dinar was worth two pounds sterling. He gave us brief directions as to how to get to the College, which was nearby, and asked us to meet him at his office at ten in the morning. 'Right, gentlemen,' he said, 'if there is nothing else I shall bid you goodnight.' George and I said we were fine, and at that Nigel smartly left the flat. George and I immediately slumped into armchairs.

'What do you think then?' I asked

'Not bad, not bad at all,' replied George.

After several minutes' silence, George said, 'What we need in here is music. Yes, music, that's what we need. I must get into town soon and see if I can pick up a little blaster,' he said. 'Fancy a coffee?'

'Yes,' I said, 'great.'

'On you go then, spot of milk and two sugars for me, please,' said George.

I was in the kitchen and waiting for the kettle to boil before I realised that I had been duped. I decided to say nothing, but told myself I would make sure that George would take his turn of making the coffees next time. George said little while he sipped his coffee.

'What do you think of Nigel, then?' I asked.

'A blithering idiot,' said George.

'What makes you say that?' I asked.

'Only an idiot calls a total stranger an idiot. Especially one who is trying to help you,' said George.

'Oh, right,' I said. 'Do you think he is going to be a bit of a problem?'

'Nah,' replied George, 'he's all right. Just a bit of a Henry, that's all.'

'He makes me think of a military man,' I said. 'Perhaps a young RAF officer.'

George did not reply.

I didn't sleep much that night. All the events and even the conversations of the day kept playing back in my mind. I could not have slept for much more than four hours when I was wakened by the sound of *Muezzins* broadcasting prayers. There were three or four *Muezzins* in the distance, which sounded like a rippling echo of the local holy man nearby. It was still quite dark and only about five o'clock, but I did not mind having my sleep interrupted this early. I enjoyed listening to the prayers. They made me acutely aware of being in a country that was very different from my own. I had been in France and in Spain on holiday, but this place seemed very different. Yes, I thought, Kuwait is different.

Chapter Two

Without opening my eyes I stretched over and silenced my small, but very loud, alarm clock. It took me several seconds to figure out where I was. Then I remembered the *Muezzins*. I opened my eyes and glanced towards the window. The sky was completely cloudless and outside seemed very quiet and still. The room was pleasantly warm and I found swinging my feet round and onto the floor no hardship at all. I bimbled towards the bathroom. The bathroom door was locked. George had beaten me to it. So, I about-turned and bimbled back again. I went to the window. The first thing that struck me was the lack of greenery. Every one of the houses and buildings I could see was either sand coloured or white, and all had flat roofs. Less than a mile a way I could see the Gulf. The sun was already blazing down. It was a delightful view. This'll make living on the sixth floor not so bad, I told myself.

Later, in the living room, George and I agreed that quarter to ten would be a good time to set out for the College. George slid deeper into his armchair and re-immersed himself in a book he had been reading, and, perhaps feeling slightly lost and restless, I made coffees, but I wished I hadn't bothered. Without even sipping his coffee, George described it as rubbish. I felt something like disappointed seeing this on my face, George immediately stated, 'It's the water, mate.'

'But, it's filtered,' I said.

'It's still rubbish,' George snapped. 'Don't worry,' he said, in a much softer tone, 'I'll get some bottled water later.' I wondered why George didn't complain about last night's coffee.

While I was in my bedroom making sure I had all the bits and pieces I would need I heard the flat door close. I had been expecting and hoping that George and I would have gone into the College together. No matter, I told myself. I left the flat, and for some reason or another, ignoring the lift, I took the stairs down. In the stairwell it was beautifully cool, and I wondered how hot it would be outside. My question was answered in no uncertain terms when I stepped out into the street. It was very hot, but not at all unpleasant. I quite liked it. As I turned towards the College I right away noticed that there were large areas of spare ground. I reasoned that these areas were probably full of houses at one time, and I found myself wishing that they hadn't been pulled down. The pavement was simply a stretch of sand, edged with a kerb. I liked this. I found it slightly amusing somehow. Some of the sand was quite soft. In no time, I was outside the College. It was a huge, white cube of a building, surrounded by a large wall in which there were large iron entry gates. It was an attractive building with a narrow balcony round the top one of its three storeys, and lots of fancy, albeit concrete features. I could see the tops of palm trees above the wall. Perfect, I thought. There were about ten, large American cars parked outside.

Nigel's office was on the first floor. George was already inside when I arrived. The office's three chairs were large and leathery. As I settled down, I glanced around. Nigel's desk was huge but, apart from a stand-up calendar and an ashtray, it was completely bare. The walls too were bare and, other than the desk and the three chairs, there was only a single filing cabinet. Not quite a sweatshop, I thought. Nigel was again wearing his lightweight tan-coloured suit. George and I had opted for shirt and tie. Nigel made no comment about this. Right away Nigel asked for our passports. We handed these over without question. Nigel explained that the College needed our passports so that it could apply for residency status for us. Nigel made the traditional speech on formally welcoming us to the College. He then gave us the usual spiel of telling us the sort of things that normally come under the heading of, 'the set-up here'. As he droned on, my mind began to wander. But I was instantly all ears when I heard him say, 'I don't mind admitting that I wear make-up.' Rather anxiously, I wondered what he was on about and was rather relieved when I remembered that he had been talking about how merciless the Kuwaiti sun could be. After no more than about ten minutes, Nigel suggested that we continue our conversation round at his local tearoom. George and I agreed that this seemed a good idea. Nigel's local tearoom turned out to be the Kuwait International Hotel.

The International was a huge hotel with a sumptuous entrance. I almost felt I was entering illegally or under false pretences in some way. The entire ground floor was marble. Two armed policemen, standing to one side, watched us as we went in. An escalator took us up to the foyer on the first floor. Here, there was a huge reception desk, a bookshop and a bank. Nigel's teashop was in fact a French-style café, with fancy mirrors on the walls and ornate side chairs at small round tables. One entire wall was a window which gave, above lots of large, leafy plants, a splendid, panoramic view of the Gulf. Nigel had a small pot of tea and a croissant. George and I opted for coffee. It was the most expensive coffee I had ever had. Nigel said he came to this little hide-away every day, and invited George and I to join him from now on. George and I looked towards each other. The expression on George's face was saying, no way, Nigel, not at these prices. And, I seemed to know that George could see the same sentiment written all over my face.

Back at the College, Nigel led us straight up to the staff room. In the room there were only women. I asked Nigel if this was everybody and he confirmed that it was, apart from Joanna, his Assistant Director of Studies. Nigel introduced us to everyone individually. There was one Egyptian woman. The rest were from various parts of the UK. Every teacher had their own desk, and Nigel asked us to share with someone until such time as he was able to fix us up with our own desk. Nigel asked us to meet him in the foyer in about fifteen minutes time. He said he wanted us to meet the boss. He pointed out and explained to me the tea and coffee arrangements in the staff room, and then left. In no time, the room had almost emptied, apart from George and I and Liz, one of the two typing teachers. George seemed to be hitting it off with Liz, so I decided to make myself a coffee, for something to do as much as anything.

'Ah,' George called out from across the room, 'while you're at it, mate. Usual spot of milk and two sugars for me, please.'

In the foyer, Nigel was waiting for us by the reception desk. He right away knocked on and opened the door marked, *Principal.* Inside, a tall man with thinning grey hair and a grey moustache immediately stood up, pushed out his right hand and introduced himself as David. We shook hands. His handshake was extremely firm. His desk was even bigger than Nigel's, and cluttered. David did little more than welcome us to the College and to Kuwait, and said he hoped we would enjoy our stay. We were in David's office for little more than five minutes. Back in the foyer, Nigel said that we had the rest of the day to ourselves. He added that the next two days, Thursday and Friday, were the weekend, and that we would not be required back at the College until Saturday morning. He asked us to pop in to see Joanna in her office about ten on the Saturday. Joanna's office was in the library, which was immediately opposite reception. Before he left, Nigel gave us brief directions to our nearest supermarket, and added that there was also an excellent shopping area at Salyma, just a few miles to the south.

When we got to the College entrance, I asked, 'What now then? Trip to the Dasmah Co-op, get some food in?'

'Eh, no, you carry on, mate. I'll catch up with you later,' said George.

I wondered what he had in mind, but I decided not to ask.

With that, George turned, went back through the foyer and disappeared upstairs. The only thing I could think of to do was go shopping on my own.

As I made my way towards the supermarket I became increasingly uneasy. I seemed to be the only person in European clothes. I felt different and conspicuous. I told myself to get a grip. There was nothing to be apprehensive about. There weren't that many people about, and nobody was giving me a second look.

As I neared the supermarket, I wondered what it would be like. I had been told that one of the worst things about being abroad for a long spell was the not being able to get one's favourite foods. From the outside the shop looked quite modern, but I assumed that inside it would be rather basic, a sort of covered market. I could hardly have been more wrong. The shop was modern and seemed at a glance to be well stocked. Essentially, it was little different from my local Sainsbury's back in London. There were very few shoppers in the place though, and there were only a handful of staff. I noticed that all the staff were males. As I wandered round I was pleasantly surprised to see that there seemed to be nothing of my normal shopping list that was unavailable. Brilliant, I whispered to myself when I saw Kit-Kats on the shelf. Discovering fish fingers in the freezer made my day. I remembered George saying he would get water, but I grabbed a couple of bottles just in case. I enjoyed my tour of the aisles, but my not being able to speak Arabic at the checkout made me feel uncomfortably foreign and inept.

I was unloading my poly bag into the fridge when the doorbell went. It was one of the teachers I had met just a couple of hours before. While I was trying to remember her name she stepped in and went and sat at the dining table. I sat opposite. She was a petite woman with chin-length blonde hair and about as neat a nose as I had ever seen. She reminded me that her name was Sally. She told me she lived in the flat below and said that she had just popped in to give me a bit of an insight into life in Kuwait. At an appropriate moment, I said to myself, offer tea or coffee. Sally mentioned things to do in Kuwait, how to get about, and where there were some good shops and some of the best buys. While Sally was talking, I nodded and smiled at what I thought were the right places. I asked Sally why there were so few male teachers at the College. This brought the hint of a smile to her face and added a subtle sparkle to her bright, deep-blue eyes.

'You men don't have the staying power,' she said.

'Oh,' I said with probably a bemused look on my face, 'what exactly do you mean?' I asked.

'Well, you and George are replacing a couple of blokes who disappeared within just a few weeks of their arrival.'

'What do you mean, disappeared?' I asked

'Packed up on the Wednesday evening and simply did not turn up for work on the Saturday,' she said. 'Just did a runner.'

'Why would they do that?' I asked.

'Well,' she said, 'if you look closely at the small print on your contract you will see that there are fairly stiff penalties for breech. So, rather than pay these fines, if people decide they want to pack the job in, they bugger off back home. Well, we just assume that that is what they do,' she said.

Sally stood up and walked towards the door. I asked her if she would like a tea or a coffee. She declined with a thank you. She said she had to hurry and that she was meeting a friend to go for a swim up at the hotel. No more than ten minutes after Sally left, George came in. He had a big smile on his face.

'Guess what?' he said, jangling a bunch of keys in front of his face.

'I give up,' I said.

'I've got some wheels,' he said.

'How come?' I asked.

'Liz is going to Bahrain for the weekend and has left me her car,' he said.

'What kind of car?' I asked.

'A Jeep,' George said.

'What, one of those little things you see in American war movies?'

'No,' George replied, 'a great big thing. A bit like an overgrown Range Rover.'

'What are you going to do with it?' I asked.

'I thought we could go for a picnic,' he said.

'Where to?'

'Out into the desert,' he said.

'The desert? Surely there is somewhere better to go than that,' I said.

'No, the desert would be great,' he insisted. 'Haven't you ever been so far out at sea that you could see no land?' I shook my head. 'Well,' George went on, 'it's a great experience. And, I reckon you could do the same out in the desert. A pile of sarnies and a few drinks, brilliant,' he said.

'When do we set off then?' I asked.

'High noon,' he said.

Next morning, George woke me about nine. I immediately started thinking about this. I had wondered whether I ought to lock my bedroom door. Now I found disturbing the thought that at any point during the night somebody could come into my room while I was fast asleep.

Knowing that George would be in the bathroom, I decided to sit on the edge of my bed for a while. The room was chilly, and I became aware of the noise of running machinery. George had switched on the air conditioning. Not at all necessary, I said to myself. I began to think about the previous day, and about Sally. Somehow I felt sure that I was going to enjoy having her as a neighbour. I thought about the disappearance of the two male teachers and wondered what it could have been that compelled them to just run like that.

My attempt to get into the bathroom was successful, but I quietly cursed George for not having given me an all-clear knock on my bedroom door. The shower was delightful. And, as I stood deliriously enjoying the heavy flow of hot water the point at which to switch off and step out became an increasingly big decision. At last, as ever, I acquired the courage to turn the water off by briefly switching off my mind to the pleasure I was having. While I was drying myself, a small dark object, partially hidden behind the pedestal of the wash-hand basin, caught my eye. I bent closer to get a better look. Realising it was an enormous cockroach sent a shiver down my spine. I immediately vacated the bathroom. In the living room, George was in his armchair, reading.

'Hey, George,' I said, 'there's a cockroach the size of a Sherman tank in the bathroom. Could you deal with it please? I'm not good at that sort of thing.'

With an irksome-sounding sigh George thumped his book onto the arm of his chair and set off towards the bathroom. He returned just a minute or so later.

'What did you do with it?' I asked. 'You didn't kill it did you?'

'What did you expect me to do?' George asked. 'Tell it in a very loud voice to pack its bags and leave immediately? No,' he continued, 'I just whacked it with my slipper and swept it into the Arab toilet. If he's a good swimmer he'll surface somewhere with little more to nurse than a severe headache, and possibly a hurt pride.'

At midday, George emerged from his bedroom and with a 'Right then, let's go,' disappeared out of the flat. He was obviously leaving it to me to bring the eats and drinks. If nothing else he is consistent – he'd also got me to make up the sandwiches last night. Before leaving I went to the thermostat on the wall by the door and tweaked it until the air conditioning went off.

As we neared the car, I asked, 'What's the plan, then?'

'No idea,' George replied. Brilliant, I thought. With one turn of the ignition key, he gave life to our huge horseless carriage.

In no time, we were cruising through what seemed to be the centre of Kuwait City. I had no idea as to what I had been expecting, but I was certainly surprised to see so many large modern buildings. One large building was painted entirely in gold. One of the very tall buildings had a front and back of deep blue glass and sides of grey/blue concrete. Another one had an edifice of entirely fancy, moulded concrete blocks. I had seen no signs of war damage until George pointed out the Sheraton Hotel to me. The hotel entrance was badly damaged and a large area above had been blackened by smoke. We continued along a modern two-lane motorway. As we progressed, the signs of civilisation got fewer and farther between. The sun was blazing down but it was comfortably cool in the car. Eventually, still on a modern highway, we were flanked on either side by nothing but desert. Without warning, and with a sharp turn to the left, George bumped us off the motorway and onto the desert.

'What are you doing?' I asked.

With an air of disdain, George replied, 'We've got an off-road vehicle here. So, let's get it off the road.'

We set off into the vast emptiness of the desert, with nothing but sand between our bonnet and the distant horizon, above us a cloudless sky. The terrain was deceptively undulating and the jeep pitched and rolled like a dinghy on a choppy sea.

'Slow down, George,' I said. 'What's the hurry?'

George's response to this was to loudly start treating me to his unique interpretation of *We're Riding Along on the Crest of a Wave.*

'You're mad,' I yelled. In response to this, George enhanced his performance by adding steering-wheel bongo drums to it. I decided to keep my mouth shut.

We pressed on. The sun beat down, making it almost painful to look at the desert sand. The surface was now pancake flat. After about ten minutes, George slowed the jeep to almost a halt, turned round and looked out the rear window. Without saying a word, he put his foot down and we set off again. Every so often, this little ritual of slowing and looking round was repeated. I could not resist any longer my asking George what this was all about. George explained that he was trying to get to a point at which there was absolutely nothing to see at all on the horizon. 'Don't be silly,' I said, 'it'll take hours to get that telecom tower out of sight. It's about a thousand feet high.'

'Let's have a little rest,' said George.

'Good idea,' I replied. 'I'll dig out some Cokes.'

Shortly after we had stopped, I turned to open my door. George immediately expressed his disapproval of this. 'Do not open that door,' he bellowed.

'Oh, I just thought as we are having a little picnic the usual thing would be to open the car door.'

'Not in this sort of environment you don't,' said George. 'Open that door and the inside of this car will be like a potter's kiln in no time.'

'But its nice and cool in here,' I protested.

'That's because the car is air-conditioned, you pillock,' said George.

'Oh, I never thought of that, I was wondering why it was so cool in here.' Posh car, I thought. 'How hot do you think it is out there, then?' I asked.

'You could fry eggs on that bonnet,' replied George.

'Oh, we slipped up there.'

'We slipped up where?'

'We could have brought some eggs.'

'Shut up.' said George.

Suddenly, George leaned forward, switched on the ignition, shot us forward, pulled and pulled at the steering wheel, taking us round in a tight circle and set us off at speed back towards Kuwait City.

'What the hell are you doing?' I yelled.

'Well,' said George, nonchantly, 'almost invariably when this sort of situation arises in the best B movies, somebody says, "We've got company".'

Company, what does he mean company? We're in the middle of the desert. 'What do you mean?' I asked.

'Look behind you,' said George casually.

Slowly I turned and looked through the car's rear window. Less than half a mile away there was a vehicle. It was coming towards us, at speed it seemed. It was closing on us, despite the fact that we were doing about sixty. 'What is it?' I asked.

'It's an armoured personnel carrier,' George replied. 'We must have crossed the Iraqi border'.

'What do you think they want?' I asked.

'I don't think we should hang about long enough to find out,' said George.

'So, what do we do?' I asked.

'Well, my gut reaction tells me to try to get the greatest possible distance between us and them in the shortest possible time,' replied George, still cooler than a cucumber.

There was a crack and a thud at the back of the car.

'What was that?' I asked.

'They hit us up the arse,' said George.

This is it, I said to myself. We're done for. I gripped the dashboard. My body was numb, my mouth dry and I stared blindly ahead. There was another crack, and the sound of a bullet whistling past my window. My heart seemed to stop. Suddenly, there was what sounded like an explosion. Oh my God, I thought, they're lobbing bombs at us now. I waited, wondering what the end would be like. George slowed and stopped the car. 'What the hell are you doing?' I yelled.

George didn't say anything. He had a strange, wry smile on his face. Oh my God, I thought, we're surrendering. I immediately imagined myself in shackles, and being beaten about the head.

At last, George said, 'Have a look.' With my mind jumping from possibility to possibility as to what I might see, I slowly turned my head. Just a few hundred yards away there was a large ball of fire on the desert floor with, above it, a pillar of thick, billowing black smoke. I turned and looked towards George.

Anticipating what was on my mind, he said, 'Hit a mine, the poor buggers.'

We set off again, now at a moderate speed. Neither of us spoke for several minutes. Suddenly, I had a horrible thought.

'Hey, George, if they hit a mine it means that we are in the middle of a mine field.'

'Yes,' George replied. 'Frightening, isn't it?'

'What are we going to do?' I asked.

'What would you like us to do?' asked George, 'Get out and tiptoe back to Kuwait City? Don't worry. We'll be alright. I'm tracing our old tracks.'

'Of course,' I said.

Why didn't I think of that? I said to myself.

The deep drone of our tyres on the concrete road back to Kuwait City was a beautiful noise. Everything was beautiful. I asked George how he managed to stay so cool in that unreal and frightening situation we had just experienced. He said he hadn't been cool at all. He was terrified. We laughed. All the way back to Kuwait City, we exchanged stories about some of the frightening experiences we'd had in the past, and laughed at every one. We even laughed about the fact that we were laughing.

Chapter Three

I was sure that I had only dozed an hour or so after my being roused by my local *Muezzin's* broadcast. I was right. But, when I opened my eyes I realised it was his midday prayers I had heard. I was annoyed with myself for wasting an entire forenoon, but I enjoyed finding a free bathroom. George was not about. While I was sitting in the living room having a bit of breakfast I thought about the previous day. Already, it seemed like a dream. I could hardly believe we had been shot at and that it hadn't even crossed our minds to report this to the police. It was as if in Kuwait one ought to half-expect one's life to be in danger from time to time, as if getting shot at was a normal part of everyday life.

I had only just entered the kitchen to put the kettle on when I heard George come in. He immediately appeared at the kitchen door, but only lingered long enough to say, 'Yes, please.' There was only enough bottled water for one cup of coffee. I thought about making George's separately with tap water, but something made me think better of this. I popped down to our local shop and picked up a couple of bottles of water. When I entered the living room George was sitting in his armchair, sifting through audiotapes. There was a large ghetto blaster on the coffee table next to his chair. I put his coffee on the table. 'What do you think?' he asked, glancing towards his new purchase.

'Not bad,' I said. But I immediately started to have doubts as to whether I was going to share in the pleasure that presumably this machine was going to bring to George. The blaster blasted out heavy metal for the rest of the day.

Next morning, while I was washing up the breakfast dishes, George shouted, 'See you over at the College, I'm off.'

By the time I got to Joanna's office, George was already there. Joanna had centre-parted, long, black hair, and smiling, intelligent, brown eyes. She introduced herself and invited me to take a pew. She welcomed George and I to the College and went on to talk about our hours, courses and various small rules and regulations. Joanna told us that the College ran Arab language and culture classes and said that Nigel was very keen that new teachers should attend these. George and I said that we would be happy to do this. She said that George and I would not actually start teaching for two or three weeks yet, and that she would ask us to help her reorganise the library system and tidy up the two book stores in the College. I would be organising things in the library such that there would be a proper lending system. George was given the task of getting things in order in the book stores. As

Joanna talked on, I began to listen less to what she was saying and more to how she was saying it. Joanna snapped me out of my dreamy state when she stood up and asked us if what she had in mind for us for the next two or three weeks was okay.

'Yes, sounds gorgeous,' I said. Joanna laughed. This made me immediately aware of what I had just said. Why do I do that? Why do I say things I don't mean to say? Joanna told us we were free for the rest of the day, and added that she would look forward to seeing us at nine in the morning. I was smiling as we were saying cheerio to Joanna but I was still angry with myself for saying something so stupid. Joanna's first impression of me is that I am a right plonker.

As we stepped into the foyer, George urged me as he had done a few days before, to carry on without him. He said he was going to pop up to the staff room to return Liz's car keys to her. I wonder what he's up to now, I said to myself.

I decided to go to the supermarket to get some bottled water, and I was glad I did. As I turned out of one of the aisles, paying more attention to a display of biscuits than I was to where I was going, I felt my trolley nudge somebody else's. It was Sally's. I apologised for my clumsiness. Her face lit up. 'Fancy being bumped into by you here,' she said. I was delighted when she suggested our going round together. With as much nonchalance as I could muster I said, 'Okay.'

Outside, as soon as we settled into a stroll towards the flats, Sally asked me what my first impressions were of Kuwait. I told her that I was already counting pints of bitter instead of sheep at night. 'I'm reading all the time,' I said.

'Well,' Sally said, 'I have a huge heap of books in my flat, so if you run out of material you know where to come. And, I've got a telly. So, if you are ever in the mood for a movie, just pop in. I'm nearly always at home in the evenings.'

I asked Sally if she could go a coffee. She said she would have to take a rain check. She had a class at midday.

I was sitting at the dining table mulling over the meeting I'd had with Joanna when George burst into the flat. He dropped heavily into his armchair. 'Stuck-up bitch!' he said.

'Who, Liz?'

'No, Joanna,' he said.

'What makes you say that?'

'Nothing really,' he replied, 'she's just stuck-up, that's all.' George had obviously fallen out with Joanna for some reason or another. I tried to get the reason out of him, but he wouldn't tell me. And when I pressed him, he simply got angry. So, I let the matter drop. But I knew for sure that something had happened between those two. George stood up, went to the air-conditioning control and, with a rather puzzled look on his face, he gazed at the dial for several seconds. He adjusted the control until the air-conditioning came on. 'Some bugger's been interfering with this,' he said. I had tweaked the knob before leaving the flat that morning, but I said nothing.

' I reckon it's that *harres*,' said George.

'How could it be him?' I asked.

'He'll have a key to all the flats,' said George.

'I didn't think of that,' I said. 'Maybe he's a spy.'

George dropped a tape into his music machine and turned the noise control up to pollution level. I retreated to my bedroom, but even with the door closed I could still hardly hear myself reading.

I made a start on my job in the library. It was painfully boring, but Joanna's popping in a couple of times boosted my morale enough to stop me continually asking myself what the hell I was doing there. At tea-break time I decided to pop up to the bookstore to see how George was getting on. The door was locked. I knocked, but there was no answer. I was about to turn away when George opened the door. Liz appeared from behind him, breezed past me with a whispery, 'Hi, Jack,' and skipped down the stairs.

'Staff room?' I asked.

‘Nah,’ he replied, ‘follow me, my son.’ He said he had found a little kiosk on spare ground just five minutes away from the College that made wonderful *falafel*.

‘Lead on,’ I said.

As we were leaving the college a voice behind us said, ’Going my way, gentlemen?’ It was Nigel. He asked if we were going to the hotel. George said that we had decided to go down-market, and told him about the little *falafel* hut.

‘Not at all,’ said Nigel ‘a class kiosk, I know it well. I’ll tag along with you chaps, if you don’t mind.’ We didn’t mind.

On the last day of our first week, while George and I were having a lunchtime snack in the flat, I asked him if he fancied popping out for a curry that evening. ‘Oh, sorry, mate, I’ve already made arrangements for tonight,’ he said. I wondered who it was, but I didn’t ask. I guessed it was Liz. ‘How are you getting on in that store room?’ I asked.

‘Not bad,’ George replied pensively. ‘You know, there’s something strange about that third floor.’

‘Oh?’

‘Yes,’ he said, ‘that floor has to be as big as the floor below and yet on the left of the landing there is only a small classroom. On the right there’s only the storeroom, which isn’t that big. So, what’s in the middle? There has to be something. But the way it looks there's nothing.'

After lunch, George's music went on so I decided to go out. I thought I would have a look around Kuwait City. Somebody had told me where there was a bus stop so I decided to check out the buses. I found the bus stop and only had a few minutes to wait. I was the only person at the stop. As the bus approached, its door folded open. It was a single deck blue and white bus. The interior was chock-a-block, so I hesitated. I was expecting the driver to say, sorry, full up. Instead, his gaze told me to gee myself. I had no idea as to the fare into town so I offered the driver a selection of coins on my palm. He picked off two small coins, and gave me a ticket that he had drawn from an elastic-banded pile by his steering wheel. I had not yet sussed the value of the small Kuwaiti coins but a rough estimate told me that the ride into town was virtually free to well-paid English teachers. Not being able to go into the bus, I turned and held onto a rail below the windscreen. The bus was purely functional but the driver immediately demonstrated that his vehicle was capable of going like the clappers. As we negotiated roundabouts and corners the bus keeled over to the left and to the right. I reasoned that the driver was probably a weekend rally driver.

Kuwait City was a bit of a disappointment. Not enough old buildings for my liking. I found the old souk, but most of it had been destroyed. Coming back from Kuwait City, because I was just a couple of stops away from the terminus, I got a seat on the bus. The trouble came later though. Getting off at Dasmah was horrendous. En route from the City, no matter how tightly packed the interior of the bus was, the driver stopped at every stop and allowed aboard everybody that was waiting. Obviously, the bus company knew exactly how many people would be waiting for a bus at every point and time on every route, and having calculated exactly the absolute maximum number of people that could be jammed into one of their buses, they were able to assure each driver that he could keep on letting people aboard happy in the knowledge that he would never exceed the maximum density of bodies that had been worked out for his bus.

I had the flat to myself this evening. I thought about knocking Sally's door, but I decided to grab the opportunity of being able to read without a heavy-metal accompaniment.

My always getting beaten to the bathroom in the morning was starting to get to me. So, I changed the setting on my alarm clock from eight o'clock to quarter to. The bathroom was invariably free by eight-fifteen, but this made getting out of the flat in time a bit of a rush.

Next morning, I strode towards the bathroom door, fingers crossed. But, yet again, the big man had beaten me to it. And, I had given myself a longer waiting time. Even earlier seemed to be the answer.

As I made my way to the College, I started looking forward to seeing Joanna. And, to my delight, when I opened the library door there she was. Even better, she wasn't busy and was clearly in a chatty mood. I discovered she was Liverpudlian and that she had been at the College for four years. Astonishingly, she had stayed in Kuwait during the Iraqi Army invasion. I asked her what it was like.

'Not too bad,' she replied.

'Weren't you terrified?' I asked.

'No, not really,' she said. 'We stayed indoors most of the time, we hardly ever saw any soldiers. We live at Salyma just a few miles south of here. There's a terrific supermarket there. We stocked up with food and things once a week and spent most of the rest of the time in my flat. I have a telly and oodles of video tapes, and we managed to keep ourselves amused one way or another.'

'We?' I asked, hoping like mad that she wasn't referring to a bloke.

'Liz and me,' she said. 'She also stayed in Kuwait during the war.'

When Joanna eventually left the office I immediately got on with my ongoing project, enthusiastically. Why am I acting so keen? I asked myself some time later. Tea break time came in no time. I leapt and bounded up to the third floor to see how George was getting on in the storeroom up there. As I neared the top stair I remembered George saying there was something weird about that floor. Before knocking the storeroom door I had a shufti at the landing. George was right, there was something strange about the place. The classroom to one side and the storeroom to the other could not be covering that entire floor, I reckoned. Partly hidden by a large cupboard, I spotted a large sheet of wood that had been attached to the wall somehow. I managed to drag the cupboard out slightly, and knocked along the wall. And, just like in the movies, at one point the noise changed.

The storeroom was unlocked. I opened it an inch or two and called inside, 'Are you there?' George emerged a few seconds later.

'I'm here,' he said.

'You're right about this floor,' I said.

'Tell me more.'

'Look at this clearly false piece of wall behind this cupboard.'

'I see what you mean, mate.'

'What do you think?' I asked.

'We'll just have to check it out,' George said.

'How?'

'I'll think of something.'

'Staff room?' I asked.

'Nah,' said George, '*Falafel* hut.'

'Okay,' I said.

George seemed to want to steer clear of the staff room. I wondered why.

As we were leaving the building, as if out of the blue, Nigel appeared.

'Going our way?' asked George.

'Well, since you asked, thank you,' said Nigel.

As we walked, and while we were sitting outside the snack place, Nigel did next to nothing but ask questions about just about everything under the sun.

Later, in the flat, I asked George about this. 'He's probably just a friendly sort of bloke, that's all', replied George. 'He probably gets lonely in that big office of his.'

'But he never tells us anything about himself,' I said. 'He only asks questions.'

'Yes, but as the Director of Studies he's the equivalent of a personnel manager,' said George. 'He's probably just concerned about our welfare. It's his job to make sure that at all times we are happy men.'

'Ah,' I said, 'I didn't think of that.'

Chapter Four

While I was wiping the worktops in the kitchen after having washed up the lunchtime dishes, I decided I would go for a stroll in the afternoon. George was popping down to Salyma with Liz, and Sally always avoided going out in the afternoon if possible. For me, it was the other way round. I hated being cooped up in the flat in the afternoons. As far back as I could remember, if the sun was shining, I had to get out. So, walkies it was.

I decided to have my stroll along the promenade by the Gulf. It was so hot that even the local mad dogs seemed to be sheltering in shaded places. After having walked about a mile of the prom my legs started to tell me it was time for a rest. I plonked my bottom down onto a low wall at the back of a popular stretch of beach near the Kuwait Towers. All over the beach, small groups of mothers and their children were having picnics. Scores of children had taken to the water. A couple of jet skis were buzzing about, but I found I could not watch them because of the way they were zigzagging to avoid the bobbing heads of a few children who had ventured out to what I felt was a rather dare-devil distance from the shore. The merciless heat of the sun had pushed two mums into taking a dip in the shallow water at the edge of the Gulf. Both were fully clothed, but no problem, I said to myself. Within an hour of their returning to the beach they would be as dry as a bone.

I had only been in Kuwait for a few weeks but already I was feeling quite settled. The flat was beginning to feel like home and I was getting on well with everybody at the College. Exasperatingly though, a few niggling little things were refusing to go away. I hated not having my passport. I described living in Kuwait to Sally one evening as feeling like serving time in a huge open prison. I said this with a chuckle but I knew I was trying to kid myself on that it wasn't troubling me. The trouble is, it was. George was getting taxis everywhere, I was sticking with the buses. I rather enjoyed travelling on the buses, but increasingly on journeys we were getting stopped by police doing spot checks. Shortly after the bus stopped, two policemen would come on board, all sub-machine gun and bandoliers of bullets. One policeman would move down the bus checking papers and passports. His having to thoroughly check these out meant that he was lingering a bit too long for my liking, and longer than normal on my document, it seemed. This was probably because I only had a photocopy of my passport. Having a loaded sub-machine gun right by my ear for what seemed like an age was a bit scary. Even the tellers at the Gulf Bank seemed to be giving me a suspicious look when I handed to them my increasingly tatty bit of paper as ID. And the mystery surrounding our not being given teaching to do. Why did they bring George and I out to Kuwait when they did, when they really didn't need us? At least, not right away. What would I not give for a pint of bitter right now? I asked myself.

The discomfort I was feeling from watching the jet skis race about among helpless young children soon became unbearable, so I resumed my stroll. When I got as far as the Kuwait Towers, which still bore evidence of soldiers having used it for target practice, I crossed the six lanes of the Gulf road and headed for home. Ahead, I could see a barrier across the pavement just at the start of the high wall that surrounded the American Embassy. There was a soldier on duty. As I neared the pavement block I decided that stepping off the pavement onto the road to pass by would be okay. But the soldier growled an order to me to get to the other side of the road. His rifle, pointing straight at me, quietly advised me not to quibble. I got home eventually.

There was quite a spring in my step as I went down to Sally's that evening. We had decided to go for a curry at a restaurant that had just newly re-opened following the war. Sally had six taxi numbers. Thus far, no matter which number we dialled, the same driver turned up. I dialled the one number that we had not yet tried but it made no difference. As usual it was Anwar in the big white Ford that came for us. I asked Sally if it had always been like this. Sally said she wasn't sure. She thought it might have been one driver for a spell, and then another driver for another spell.

The food at the Maharajah was excellent, but sparkling water in a stemmed glass was no substitute for a fine wine. Apart from savouring the wine itself, to my mind, gradually getting more and more tipsy towards the end of the meal was an essential part of eating out. Throughout the meal, Sally and I chatted and joked and laughed, just as we more or less always did when we were together.

In the taxi on the way home the patter continued. At the same time, I was thinking about where the relationship between Sally and I might be heading. She seemed to enjoy my company as much as I enjoyed hers. She had popped in to see me in my flat several times and I had spent a couple of evenings watching the telly in her flat. She never once objected to my asking her out, and she always said yes. It seems we are going to be close friends. The trouble is, I thought, when that happens there's no way back. You can't suddenly try to get things romantic if you end up good friends. Maybe romance isn't on the cards anyway. I suppose the best idea is just to wait and see what happens.

It was in the lift on the way up to Sally's flat that I thought of a little ploy. At this point when we had been out before, Sally did not ask me in for coffee. Tonight, I'll invite her up to my flat. My asking could be telling, I reasoned. But it wasn't. At her door, when I sensed that Sally was about to say good night, I quickly blurted out my invitation. She declined. She said she had a class at nine in the morning. When we said good night she kissed me on the corner of my mouth. What did all that mean? I asked myself, as I slowly climbed the stairs up to my flat.

On entering the flat, I went straight to bed. As usual I set my alarm. In my efforts to get to the bathroom before George in the mornings, I had been getting up earlier and earlier. I decided that quarter-past seven was as early as I was going to go. If I don't beat him to it at that time, I'll give up. If it means that getting out on time in the morning is a bit of a rush, so be it. Last thing I remember that night was my counting glasses of wine as well as the usual pints of bitter.

When I opened my eyes in the morning I cursed. It was ten to eight. I must have switched off my alarm and dozed off. Despite my expecting my journey to be futile, I got up right away and headed off to the bathroom, in my usual pre-ablution daze. Sure enough, he'd beaten me to it again. The door was locked. I turned and started to shuffle down the hall

and back to my bedroom. George strode pass me going the other way.
'Good morning,' he said.
'Good morning,' I replied. My mouth had opened and I had taken a breath to say, sorry, it's busy, when I froze in disbelief. 'Hey!' I yelled. Anything else I might have wanted to say would have been drowned out by George's loud laughter. The laughter continued as he unlocked and opened the bathroom door. I was gob-smacked. The crafty sod must have snaffled the bathroom key the day we moved in. It had never once occurred to me that the bathroom might be lockable from the outside.

Later, as I stepped into the library, Joanna greeted me with a chirpy, 'Good morning,' and a broad smile. What have I done to deserve this? I asked myself.
'Guess what?' Joanna said.
I pretended to be thinking.
'I give up,' I said.
'I managed to slot you into next week's schedule,' she said.
Joanna and I chatted for quite some time, firstly about teaching in general and then about our own experiences. Joanna sat casually on the edge of her desk. I was over the moon. When Joanna left the library I got stuck in, almost enthusiastically, to numbering and logging the two shelves of books that

still had to be done. While I was working, I thought about Sally and Joanna.

I loved being in Sally's company. I loved her bubbliness and her warmth. She was witty and intelligent. Sally made me feel good and happy. My feelings towards Joanna were quite different. My attraction to Joanna was entirely physical. There was something about Joanna that was almost magnetic. When I was near her I felt myself being drawn even closer. I loved the shine in Joanna's hair and the kindness in her eyes, her soft voice and her perfect skin. Joanna's presence was exciting and slightly breathtaking. I had asked around, but I still didn't know whether there was a man in Joanna's life. This was purely to satisfy my curiosity. I had absolutely no chance with Joanna. The man Joanna would settle down with would be a somebody. In no time, it was teatime.

I went to see George. I knew he would be in the portakabin storeroom in the College grounds. When I got there I stepped straight inside. George was sitting reading the Gulf Times, Liz was in the middle of moving a pile of books. George told me to make my way over to the *Falafel* hut by myself and that he would probably catch me up later. Instead, I went up to the staff room. And I was glad I did. I spent the entire break with Sally, and Joanna popped in briefly. What the hell have I been doing going over to the snack shack with George? I asked myself.

Later, Sally and I went to the supermarket together. Later still, we had a bit of late lunch in Sally's flat. As always, I wanted to go out for the afternoon. After we had washed up the lunchtime dishes I asked Sally if she fancied a wander round the shops of Kuwait City. To my delight she said yes. It was too hot to walk a distance that would have taken a good half hour and I was not about to suggest taking a bus. So, I phoned a taxi. As usual it was Anwar who came for us. In town, we only window-shopped but it was fun. Sally's endless comments on the things that were on display had me constantly chuckling. I wanted the day to last as long as possible so, in the taxi on our way home, I asked Sally if she would like to go out for a meal later. I suggested the Chinese restaurant that George had recommended to me. For a few seconds she looked pensive and said nothing. I wondered if this was because we didn't normally go out on a midweek evening. At last, she said, 'I can't make it tonight. Well, I could but it would be too much of a rush. I would have to be back by nine and that would spoil the evening slightly. This is the night I phone Stuart,' she said.

'Stuart?' I asked.

'Yes, my fiancé,' she replied.

My mouth went temporarily out of order. Seemingly, having correctly interpreted the 'your what?' expression on my face, Sally continued, 'Haven't I mentioned Stuart? I was sure I had. I must have done,' she said. Inside I was saying, no you didn't, no you didn't, while at the same time trying to look dead cool. 'Yes,' I said, 'you probably did. I have a terrible memory.'

I decided to skip my Arabic class that evening. More often than not it comprised only George and I, but we invariably met somebody, and I didn't feel like meeting people. Joanna had given George and I the rest of the week off to prepare our lessons. That's what I'll do, I thought to myself. I was feeling a strong urge to do something. I had only just got my books and a notepad out when I heard the front door close. About a second later I heard the air conditioning come on and George cursing the *harres*. Less than a minute after that, George's music came on. I tried to get into my books but I found I couldn't. I went through to the living room and asked George to turn down the volume. 'Sure, mate,' he said. Back in the bedroom I realised he turned the noise back up again. I tried hard to work but it was impossible. I went through to the living room again, and this time I went straight to George's blaster and turned the volume down myself. I didn't say a word to George. Within minutes of my returning to my bedroom the music went back to its original loudness. I felt myself getting angry. I strode through to the living room once more but this time, as I approached the radio cassette, George stood up and pushed me. I staggered backwards. Now, I was extremely angry. I found myself lunging forward. I was growling. My right fist flew towards George's face. I don't know if it connected. Suddenly, the room was spinning. The next thing I remember was my trying to figure out where I was. I could feel myself lying on a hard surface. I opened my eyes. George was peering down at me with a silly grin on his face. 'What happened?' I asked.

'You seemed to have had a rush of blood to the head, old mate,' George replied. 'So, I just shook you about a bit. That's usually the best way to get excess blood out of the bonce,' he said.

I got up and without saying a word slunk off to my bedroom. I sat at my desk fully intending to carry on with what I had been doing, but I couldn't concentrate even though George had switched off his blaster. I turned in early that night.

Next morning, I woke before my alarm went off. I got up right away and was on my way to the bathroom when my thinking cleared. I stopped. Since having had his crafty trick with the key sussed, George continued as if obsessively to beat me to the bathroom in the morning by getting up very early. Is this going to be another futile journey? I asked myself. I swithered and dithered for several moments. Then, for some reason I decided to carry on. When I grasped the bathroom door handle it turned. I thought I was imagining this. I pushed the door. It opened. I stood for a moment while taking in what had just happened. Getting straight into the bathroom was a sheer delight. I hope George is okay, I thought. I was showered, squeaky clean and had started brushing my teeth when I heard George try thc bathroom door. He shouted to me to get a move on. He's all right, I said to myself.

Joanna had told George and I to spend the days prior to our taking classes working on our own, either in the staff room or at home. We opted for the flat. I had been working at my desk for about an hour when I heard George's music coming on. But, it was so low I could hardly hear it.

Later, while I was sitting half daydreaming and half wondering what to do in the afternoon, Sally popped in. She asked me if I fancied a shufti round the shops in Kuwait City. I certainly didn't want to go into Kuwait City.

'I don't think I fancy the City today, Sally,' I said.

'Salyma?' she said.

'I don't think I fancy Salyma either,' I replied.

'The beach? What about the beach?'

'Fine, but what about all that exposure to the sun, Sally? Could you bear that?'

'Oh, I'll be alright,' said Sally. By the way, I've got cans of alcohol-free lager in my fridge. We can take them with us.'

'Well, if you're sure?' I asked.

Sally immediately got up and skipped out of the flat. I said I would catch up with her in a minute or two. I began to hope Sally would be okay out in the afternoon sun. Sally had very fair skin. I wondered why she was willing to take the risk of making herself ill by going outdoors today. She'll probably put on a high factor sun cream. I wondered why I hadn't told Sally the real reason as to why I didn't want to go in to Kuwait City. Travelling on the buses was starting to get to me. Every bus I caught now was getting stopped and checked. When the police came aboard the atmosphere got really tense. I kept imagining that an unconscious movement of my hand to just scratch my face or my head could be misconstrued and be my last move. I kept looking forward to the end of the Government clampdown on illegal immigration.

The beach was deserted. I wondered why. Sally explained that it was because it was a school day. And, before long mothers and children began to trickle onto the beach. By mid-afternoon the beach was full of life. Sally and I were sitting at the back of the beach. We chuckled as we watched the toddlers waddle their way down to the water's edge. We munched crisps and guzzled the lager. It was a wonderful afternoon, but the alcohol-free lager was mind-boggling.

I thought I'd better show my face at the Arabic class. George and I walked together over to the College. As soon as we stepped into the foyer, Ebtisan, the receptionist, directed us to the classroom on the third floor. Apparently somebody had commandeered our usual room. During the lesson I noticed a second door in the classroom. If it wasn't a cupboard, which I was sure it wasn't, it had to be an access door into the secret room. At the end of the lesson I held back and beckoned to George. We tried the door. It was locked.

'This proves that there is a room that has been sealed off,' I said.

'It sure does,' said George.

'What shall we do?' I asked.

'We check it out,' said George.

'How do we do that?'

'We break in, pillock.'

'But, it would be a hell of a job breaking this door down. We would be heard all over the College.'

'Pillock. When you wish to make an illicit entry into a building you don't go breaking bloody doors down.'

'How do you get in then?' I asked.

'You enter stealthily though a window,' said George.

'But there are no windows in that room,' I said. 'I've checked it out. There are only the windows of this room and the storeroom, which are at the side of the building. There are no windows at the back of the College on the third floor.'

'And that means just one thing,' said George.

'What's that?'

'Are the little brain cells not collaborating well tonight, my son?' asked George. 'It means there's a window in the roof.'

'How can you be so sure?' I asked.

'No Arab house is ever designed such that one room needs artificial lighting on during the daytime,' said George.

'Fascinating,' I said. 'How did you know that?'

'I didn't,' said George. 'I just thought it would sound good.'

'How do you get onto the roof?' I asked.

'The ancient Egyptians invented an apparatus that proved to be a great boon to the window cleaning industry,' said George. 'They called it a ladder.'

I was sure George's story about the history of the ladder was another whopper, so I decided to try to catch him out about the windows. 'Did the ancient Egyptians have windows, then?'

'Windows? Double-glazing, mate,' said George. I decided to ask no further history questions.

'So, where do we get a ladder long enough to reach all the way up to the roof of the College?' I asked.
'We don't need one,' replied George, 'we only need one that'll reach from the third floor balcony.'
'Okay, but how do we get it through the building and up to the third floor?'
'Trust me, my son. Leave it to me.'
'Have we got such a ladder?' I asked.
'Yes, there's one in the outside storeroom.'

George and I were sitting in the living room and he was reading as ever. I was day-dreaming.
'I'm popping down to the Sultan Centre, in Salyma,' said George. 'Why don't you tag along?'
'Oh, right, thank you,' I said. 'I think I will.'
We walked round to the Kuwait International Hotel to get a cab. Most of the cars in Kuwait were American, but very modern and just like overgrown British cars. The car that happened to be at the front of the taxi rank was one of the older, unmistakably American cars. Huge. A bonnet the size of a tennis court and a boot you could have held pop concerts in. As we floated along I felt like a film star. This is the life, I kept saying to myself. In next to no time we were pulling up outside the Sultan Centre. While I was paying the driver, George went in search of a trolley. Inside the foyer of the supermarket, George passed the trolley to me. I asked him about his own shopping. He said that he would put his stuff in my

trolley. Something told me that at the checkout, I would be paying for the entire contents of this trolley. We started off in the fruit and veg section. As I fussily inspected and selected onions and then potatoes, George kept disappearing and reappearing with tins and packets, and dropping them into the trolley. I was slowly browsing my way along the vegetables when I spotted a gorgeous-looking bunch of broccoli. As I reached for it, my hand was pipped by another hand.

'Oops, sorry,' I said. The reply was a chuckle. I looked to my side. It was Joanna. We laughed.

'I'm just about finished,' said Joanna. 'How about you?'

Something told me a suggestion was coming up, so although I had only just started and had only a few of items in my trolley, I said, 'Yes, me too.'

'My flat is just around the corner. Fancy a coffee?' asked Joanna.

'Brilliant,' I said.

'Shall we meet in the foyer?' Joanna asked.

'Fine,' I replied.

I looked around but couldn't see George anywhere. I raced round and grabbed as many things as I could think of. At the checkout, as if from nowhere, George appeared. I paid for the shopping. At the other side of the checkout, I told George about Joanna's invitation and suggested he might be welcome to come along.

'Nah,' he said, 'I've got better things to do. Have fun.' As he spoke he ruffled my hair and with a chuckle turned and walked away. Oh no, I said to myself, he hasn't, has he? I checked. He has. I can't let Joanna see me like this, I said to myself.

I had plenty of hair, but there was no denying the fact that I had the dreaded receding hairline. I hated it. It was just so uncool. And, since I had thick hair on the top, using this to cover the thin hair at the front seemed the obvious thing to do. Over the years though, it had all become a little bit of an obsession. I hated windy days. And, everywhere I went I made a beeline for a toilet or a bathroom to check in the mirror that the cover-up was in place.

I desperately scanned the foyer for a toilet and sighed a huge sigh of relief when I spotted one just beyond the last checkout. Brilliant. But, I had taken just two steps towards it when I was stopped dead in my tracks by a 'yoo-hoo.' I turned round. It was Joanna. 'Right then, let's go,' she said.

'I'm afraid I've lost George or perhaps he has lost me,' I said.

'Oh, forget him, you'll be okay.'

Every time Joanna glanced towards me as we walked and chatted I felt sure she was looking at my hair. Joanna's flat was on the second floor of a four-storey block. On entering the flat we went directly to the kitchen. I parked my poly bag and asked Joanna if I could help her put her shopping away.

She said she was fine and told me to go on through. I asked her if she would mind my using her bathroom. 'Of course not,' she said.

The bathroom was large, fully tiled and entirely pink. While I was rearranging my hair, I noticed a plastic tumbler on the mirror shelf and decided to have a drink of water. I had only taken a sip when the tumbler slipped from my hand, bounced on the edge of the wash-hand basin, emptied half its contents onto my trousers and fell to the floor. For a minute I stood stunned, immediately knowing that I had given myself a huge problem. Think positively, I told myself. I drew off a couple of yards of toilet paper and vigorously rubbed my trousers but this helped little. The huge damp patch remained horribly obvious on my light-coloured trousers. A woman's magazine on top of a bath stool caught my eye. This'll have to do, I said to myself. Using the magazine to cover the damp patch, I went through to the living room. In the room, there was a four-seater settee, a couple of armchairs and an easy chair. I opted for the settee, and sank into one end of it with the magazine on my lap. Soon, Joanna came in.

'Kettle's on,' she said. She walked over to her balcony doors. 'Have you seen my fantastic view of the Gulf?' She opened one of the windows. 'There you go,' she said, 'grab a seat on the balcony for a few minutes while I make the coffees.' Unable to think of what else I could do, I stood up and took the magazine with me.

'Oh, I am sorry,' said Joanna. 'I've left you stuck with that mag.' When she moved towards me with her hand outstretched I knew I had no choice but to hand the magazine to her. She noticed my predicament right away.

'Oh, you poor dear, you've had a little accident,' she said.

'Yes,' I said with a laugh. 'It was in the bathroom.'

'Obviously,' Joanna said.

'No, no,' I said, 'It's not what you think. I spilled a glass of water.'

'Oh, yes,' Joanna said, probably doubting my story. 'Well, you can't stay in those clothes,' she said. 'That must be right through to your underwear. They'll have to come off.'

'No, it's all right. I'll be fine, honestly.'

'Don't be silly,' Joanna said. 'I'll give you a towel to put round you.'

'No, honestly, I'll be all right,' I protested.

'Well if you refuse to remove that wet clothing, there's only one thing for it. Wait right there,' Joanna said firmly. She then left the room. She returned just a minute or so later carrying a huge hairdryer. 'Over you come,' she said, crouching to plug in the dryer.

My mind immediately went back to my clumsy childhood days, when my mother would make me stand still while she wiped chocolate from around my mouth or ice cream from the front of my shirt. Joanna switched on the hairdryer and directed the hot air to the front of my trousers.

'Let me know if that gets too hot,' she said. 'I don't want your balls to start baking.' I laughed out loud.

Then, still chuckling, I said, 'Well, I am hoping to have a long future of needing them in an uncooked state.'

Later, sitting right next to me on the settee, Joanna treated me to a feast of delightful anecdotes and brilliant, thought-provoking observations. I kept having to pinch myself. Just an hour before, and for weeks, I had perceived Joanna as a woman that would never be more than a colleague and an acquaintance. And now here we were, sitting on this settee in her flat, chatting like old friends. I couldn't figure out why Joanna had apparently taken a shine to me, but I was not about to get any big ideas. Almost inadvertently it seemed, Joanna mentioned George's name.

'By the way, what gives with you two?' I asked. 'You seem to be the best of enemies. And it seems to me you have never given yourselves the chance to get to know each other.'

'Well, I certainly do not dislike George. But he certainly seems to be in a huge huff with me.'

'Why is that, do you think?' I asked.

'I'm not at all sure,' replied Joanna. 'But it may well be because I turned him down when he asked me out.'

'He asked you out, did he?'

'Yes, on the first day we met.'

Ah, that's it, I said to myself. He hasn't been avoiding the staff-room, he's been avoiding Joanna.

'Why did you knock him back?'

'I seemed to know right away that George wasn't my type, and I didn't want to give him the wrong idea. Had we become friends first, I probably would have gone out with him.'

'How could you be so certain about him?' I asked.

'Oh, I've always been able to tell almost instantly who is and who is not my type.'

'What is your type, then?'

'The type who can put up with a bossy-boots,' said Joanna, laughing.

'Are you a bossy-boots?'

'I could teach a sergeant major the tricks of the bossing-people-about trade,' said Joanna.

'You don't come across to me that way at all,' I said.

Like all good things, my amazing afternoon came to an end. Joanna was working that evening. She gave me a lift back to Dasmah. On the way we chatted about family and friends back home. It soon became fairly clear that Joanna was not in a relationship. Despite my knowing well that this made no difference at all as to how Joanna perceived me, for some reason it made me something like glad to know that she wasn't in love with somebody.

As soon as I entered the flat, George emerged from his bedroom. Right away he asked me how I'd got on in the afternoon. Suddenly feeling mischievous I simply said, 'Not bad'.

'Did she say anything about me?' he asked. I knew exactly what George was fishing for, but the devil in me decided to let him go on suffering over this. He started almost begging me to tell him more, but I insisted there was nothing to tell.

'Right, get a move on,' said George. 'We've got work to do this evening.'

'What work?' I asked.

'We've got to get a ladder from the outside storeroom up to the third floor balcony.'

But we'll be seen,' I said.

'We wait till after seven when all the classes have started. By that time most of the teachers and students will be out of the way. If anybody does see us, we just put on a purposeful look, as if we're doing something we're supposed to be doing.' How do you look purposeful, I asked myself?

I had a quick snack while George listened to Arabian music on the Kuwait radio station. He obviously hadn't given up trying to get more out of me about my afternoon with Joanna.

'Reckon you're in there then, mate?' he asked.

'No way,' I replied. 'Joanna is well out of my class.'
'Oh, I don't know, she's nothing special,' George said.
'She gorgeous,' I protested.
'She's fat,' George said.
'She's not fat, she's well built.'
'That's a euphemism for fat.'
'She's cuddly.'
'Another euphemism.'
'Okay, she's plump.'
'Fat.'
'Joanna's dress size is irrelevant anyway,' I said. 'She's gorgeous.'
'You're in love with her, you fool,' said George.
'I don't have a snowball in hell's chance with Joanna,' I said.
'That may be so, ate, but that doesn't stop you being daft about her,' George said.
I couldn't think of an answer to that, so I said nothing.

George had a key to both the outdoor and the third floor storerooms. We collected the ladder first. It was a straight, runged ladder and not very long. George assured me that it would reach from the balcony to the roof. As we went through the foyer, Ebtisan was looking at us from her desk. She had a rather bemused look on her face. I told her we were going up to change a couple of light bulbs upstairs. Why do I invariably in these situations come out with a statement of crap? I asked myself. On the way up the stairs, I wondered whether a runged ladder could be wedged in between floor and ceiling so that it could be used to change a light bulb. We had no trouble in getting the ladder up the stairs, through the storeroom, out of the glass door and onto the balcony. We left the ladder there, and made a slightly late entry into the Arabic class.

The Arabic class finished at nine, which left us at least an hour to kill before the College would be empty and locked for the night. We agreed that it would be unwise to be seen anywhere in the College from now on, let alone in the staff-room. So, we went into the storeroom and locked the door. There was only one chair in the storeroom so I decided to pace up and down. George warned me not to be seen at the windows or at the glass door. I sat on the floor. The time dragged. George went through with me the plan he had worked out, and got me to confirm that I was clear as to what I would be doing. At long last, with a glance at his watch, George said it was time to go. The street on that side of the College was deserted. 'Perfect,' said George.

George put the ladder in place and went up first. By the time I got onto the roof George was crawling on his hands and knees, looking from side to side and feeling around with his hands. It was quite dark on the roof but I could see reasonably well. George was obviously searching for the window that he had said earlier had to be there. Before long, I heard George say, 'Got it. It's under this tarpaulin, somewhere.' As instructed, I checked the dimly lit street below. All was quiet. George crawled on, very slowly. There was a snap and a crack. 'Oh-oh,' said George. Suddenly, bang went the window and with a shout of 'Shit!' George crashed out of sight, taking the tarpaulin with him. Oh my God, I said to myself, I hope he's all right. I stayed perfectly still and listened. Thankfully, just a few seconds later, I heard George's voice whisper loudly a string of what seemed to be thoughtfully chosen expletives. Thank God for that, I said to myself, he's okay. A pillar of light appeared above the newly created hole in the roof. I crawled towards it and peeped over the edge. 'Bloody hell, look at this,' I heard George say. The entire window frame had gone down, so there was no broken glass to worry about. Gripping the edge tightly, I swung my legs over and slowly and carefully lowered myself until I was at full stretch. I dropped into the room below. The floor was covered with broken glass and bits of window frame. I crunched my way towards George.

George immediately swung round. 'What the hell are you doing?' he bellowed.

'I thought I would come down to give you a hand,' I said.

'And where's the bloody ladder?' he growled.

'Oh,' I said. 'I forgot about that.'

'How the hell do we get out of here now, pillock?' George yelled.

I still didn't know exactly what pillock meant but somehow I seemed to know that the term accurately described the sort of person that I was currently feeling an affinity with. A rather unpopular person.

We wandered round the room. There was what looked like a fairly large printing press, a computer that George described as a desktop publishing system, two PCs with printers, a guillotine, lots of card and paper and a shelf of inks. Clearly this was a high-class, and presumably a once busy, print room.

'I think we've seen enough,' said George. 'Let's get out of here.'

'How?' I asked.

'Well, that door there is the one that's sealed off. Therefore this door is obviously the one that leads into the small classroom. So, I reckon this one would be considerably easier to make an escape through.'

'But it's locked,' I pointed out.

'So it is. But the lock is on the inside. So, give me your Swiss army knife,' said George.

'How did you know I had a Swiss army knife?'

'You're a Swiss army knife type of bloke,' George said.

'Oh, right,' I said.

George unscrewed the lock and placed it on a bench by the door. Stepping into the classroom we simply pulled the door closed behind us. Fortunately, the main classroom door was unlocked. As we were about to start down the stairs, I asked George about the ladder. He snarled a bit but I was sure he was glad that I had remembered it. George unlocked the storeroom door. We went straight through and onto the balcony. George lifted the ladder, turned it horizontally and launched it straight over the railing. It floated down and landed with a heavy splat just outside the outside storeroom. In the foyer, we opened a window and had no trouble in climbing out and onto the huge porch in front of the College. There was now only the front gate to negotiate. We climbed up, over the top, and were lowering ourselves to drop when a voice behind us said, 'Hello.' We dropped to the ground and looked round. It was a policeman, complete with sub-machine gun, the shiny bits of which were glinting in the faint light from a nearby street lamp. He asked to see our papers. Without a word, I handed over my tatty photocopy. He studied it for a minute or two. I doubted whether he would be able to read any of it in the near-darkness. He handed it back to me and turned to George. As George handed over his papers he told the policeman we were teachers and that we had been accidentally locked in the College through working late. He told the policeman that after the end of his lesson he had started a print run on his computer, that had this print run been stopped it would have been ruined, that his colleague here generously offered to stay with him, and that the print run was very important. As George waffled on, the expression on the policeman's face got more and more pained. As the policeman returned George's photocopy, sounding utterly exasperated he said, 'Okay'. He then turned, raised one arm and said, 'Goodbye,' and strode off.

We did not go home directly. George said the policeman may well be sneakily watching us from some dark place. We went down the street by the side of the College, across an area of spare ground and round the back of our block. We hurriedly entered the flats and, ignoring the lift, went straight up the stairs.

In the flat, we sat in silence for several minutes. Then, we laughed. When we calmed down, George asked me to make some coffee. I hesitated and complained that every time we had coffee together it was me that made it. George said that he asked me because the coffee he made was dreadful and that I was an expert. I started to think that maybe I ought to be proud of my coffee-making skills and that perhaps I should use this skill more willingly. After coffee, we again sat in quiet contemplation for a while. George broke the silence with, 'What did you think of that, then?'

'Well, you know, having now thought about it, as you say, I really do make an excellent coffee.'

'No, not the coffee,' said George. 'The print room.'

'Oh,' I said, 'very strange. Very strange indeed. But what I am concerned about is what might happen when the damage is discovered. I think we should steer clear of the College for a few days until things die down.'

'No, that's just what we do not do,' said George. We go over to the College, be seen and look cool. Also, we go into the staff room every day and listen out for any buzzes that might be going round. And, look surprised or puzzled as appropriate, if and when any news about the break-in breaks.'

'Of course,' I said, 'you're right.'

We called it a night about half-past twelve.

Next morning in the staff room, I asked Sally and Joanna if there was any sort of news about anything. Sally said not really, Joanna simply said no.

That evening after our Arabic class, I checked the side door of the print room. It was locked. Something fishy is going on in this place, I said to myself. Somebody, clearly having discovered that this door has been forced open, has repaired it and has kept quiet about it. Why?

In the College the following day it was again business as usual. The repaired door meant that at least one person in management knew about the print room break-in, and yet, still nothing was being said. Why didn't Nigel or David call a staff meeting and ask if anybody had seen anything unusual in the College recently, or if anybody had seen a stranger or perhaps two in or around the College? George's attitude was that he and I had solved the mystery of the sealed room and that we should now forget all about it. I needed more answers.

After lunch that day, I popped down to see Sally. I was keen to ask her about how she felt about her job and the College. She was in. I asked her how she was, then went straight onto the point of my visit. 'Tell me something, Sally,' I asked, 'do you have any concerns about your job or about the College?'

'No, not really.'

'Is there nothing about the College that you feel suspicious about?'

'No.'

I asked what she thought about Nigel. 'He seems alright,' she said.

'But he never seems to do anything,' I said. 'He just creeps about the place. His desk is always empty.'

'That's probably because Joanna does her job so well that there's next to nothing left for him to do.'

'Don't you think he looks and sounds like a military man?' I asked.

'Now that you mention it, yes, I could imagine him in a uniform.'

I asked Sally what she thought of the College's policy of taking passports from new members of staff and holding onto them for months. She said she thought this was something to do with the College having to submit passports at the right time and in a batch to the immigration people.

'Are you comfortable with that?' I asked.

'Yes, I had no problems with that because I had no reason for wanting to leave the country in my first few months. And, I now have my residency.'

Sally was obviously quite happy with everything. I still wasn't, not by any means.

Late that night as I was getting undressed for bed, I happened to drift towards my bedroom window. There were several street lamps in the area but they were faint and it was quite dark outside. I was about to turn away when something caught my eye. Through the veil of half-darkness I thought I could see people on the roof of the College. I called George through. 'Have a look towards the College,' I said. 'Do you see what I see?'

'What do you see?'

'On the roof of the College.'

'On the roof of the College I see...ahh, two blokes.'

'What do you think?' I asked.

'I think they're repairing the window.' George replied.

'Strange or what?'

'Strange,' said George. 'Very strange, but this changes nothing and we do not ask any questions. Apt questions could be answers to somebody who is secretly investigating the break-in.'

Later, in bed, I kept thinking about the print room. Why such a well-equipped print room? What was the College using it for? Why are they now trying to keep its existence a secret? I ran through in my mind the things that had happened. I remembered George asking me for my knife. I wondered what sort of bloke a Swiss army knife sort of bloke was. Did he really know that I would have a knife? Or, was he just being facetious and made a very lucky guess? With George, you never really know about anything.

I couldn't stop thinking. My two brain cells were obviously in a chatty mood. They wanted answers and were clearly not about to settle for anything less than the facts. I felt certain there was something not right about the College. I felt that it was just that I couldn't see it. Why would a College cover up a break-in and seemingly make no attempt to catch the perpetrators of this very serious crime? Why did they bring George and I out to Kuwait when they did, when there was next to nothing for us to do? And this business of always getting the same taxi driver no matter what number we dial. That's creepy. Anwar's got to be some sort of spy. The *harres* too, he always seems to be snooping round the flats. And, it wouldn't surprise me if their retaining our passports was totally unnecessary. I'm sure it really is just to stop us leaving the country. Surely they could ask us for our passports when the immigration department calls for them. Should I put up with being held like a prisoner? I wonder where they actually keep the passports?

Chapter Five

There were some things about Kuwait I loved and other things I was beginning to hate. I loved being welcomed almost every new day by a perfectly clear blue sky. I Also loved the constant sense of history I felt. The Arab dress, the mosques, the haunting echoing voices of the *muezzins* that regularly filled the Kuwaiti air. There was something I loved about living on top of a desert. I sometimes wondered if I had somehow inherited from very distant ancestors a faint memory of a life that was lived in and around the Red Sea and the Gulf. But of course my most immediate and most powerful memories were those of my life back home. I missed the simple things like trees, green fields and rolling hills. I also missed entertainment. And I missed the pints of carefree decadence that were cheerfully and regularly served by my local landlady. I missed too sitting in the garden in the summer and being warmed by the look and heat of a log fire in the winter.

George bought a small telly but apart from the odd American movie there was nothing else to watch but news. Despite this, if we were in, the telly was on. After discovering a telephone socket under our dining table, George got the *harres* to get us a phone. But the valuable asset status of this suffered a steep decline when we realised, as we had always known, that there was nobody to phone but the taxi companies.

What to do? I felt I had to do something. Throughout every day now I found myself agonising about the abnormal situation I felt I was now in. I was certain there was something going on at the College. I knew this was just a gut reaction, but I could not get rid of it. I reasoned that my mind would be eased if I did not have this feeling of being held in Kuwait. This meant getting my passport back. I decided to have a chat with Joanna.

In the morning, I popped over to see Joanna. I asked her if I could have a word with her. She said of course I could, and asked me what was on my mind. I asked her if the College's policy of holding onto our passports prior to our application for residency was absolutely necessary. Joanna said as far as she knew there was no hard and fast rule and nothing actually in writing that stated that passports had to be retained. She said that holding the passports meant that they would be ready at a moment's notice to be taken by David over to the immigration authority, and that this kept the College on the right side of the immigration people. I asked Joanna if she was saying that if I were to go to David and demand my passport he would have no legal reason to refuse. She said she probably was but this was just legally and in theory. If you were to ask David for your passport he would state that the College had no ulterior motive for retaining passports, that the reason for holding onto passports was fully explained in your contract and that the College could not afford to get on the wrong side of a government department. If you were to insist, David would simply argue, and keep on arguing, that you don't need your passport. I asked Joanna if all this meant that I would not be getting my passport for another couple of months yet. She nodded. Joanna said that the subject of passports had been raised at two recent management meetings. A couple of the primary school teachers had complained that without their passports they felt vulnerable. But she said David would not budge. He argued that if teachers were ever challenged they merely had to refer the police to the College. For no real reason, and half-jokingly, I asked Joanna if the passports were held in an impregnable vault at some secret location. 'Not at all,' she said, 'David keeps them in the safe in his office. Why are you so keen to get your hands on your passport, anyway?'

'I feel like a prisoner in this place'.

'And what difference would having your passport make?'

'I'd be able to pop home'.

'Between now and the end of the academic year, in August, you will only have weekends free. Are you saying you would spend five hundred quid for just a few hours at home? Is there anything or anybody in the UK that's that important?'

'No, not really.'

'Do you have enough money to pay for a return flight to the UK?'

'Not at the moment, but I should have at the end of this month, or just about enough.'

'Okay, let's say at some point you get really down. You go into David's office and jump up and down until he cracks and gives you back your passport. You pop home to the UK. When you come back, what's the situation now? You've got your passport but now you don't have the wherewithal to go anywhere. You're in a prison again, but this time it's more like a high-security establishment.'

'Well, I just want to feel that at least in theory I could pop home. Anyway, why are you being so negative?'

'I'm not being negative, I'm just being realistic.'

'Well, if things got really bad I would just resign.'

'Could you afford to do that?'

'Afford? In what sense?'

'In the money sense. Have you read your contract?'

'Yes. Well, no, not really.'

'Well if you read the small print you will find that if you resign before the end of your contract you're in breech. And the penalty for this is having to repay your last month's salary and the cost of your flight out to Kuwait.'
'Of course, I'd forgotten about that,' I said.
'Then, you have the cost of your flight back to the UK. Could you afford all that?'
'Not now, and probably not before the end of my contract.'
'Well, please try to be patient. Now that you're teaching, a couple or three months will pass quickly. Then, you'll have your passport and the feeling you want, at least in theory, of being able to go home, and when you wanted to.'
'Yes, of course, you're right'.

As I walked slowly back to the flat I replayed the conversation I'd just had with Joanna. She was right. But this didn't help me. This was unusual. I normally went away from Joanna with a spring in my step and with a fresh and positive outlook on life. Maybe this time my concerns were just too deep. My passport was official confirmation of my identity. And, in a foreign land I felt I had to have this. Without my passport I felt like a displaced person, a stereotype, one of a category. I dreaded just the thought of authority figures doubting that I was who I was saying I was. Nigel told me as he was relieving me of my passport that the police had assured the College that photocopies would be acceptable. But, did every policeman and soldier know this? And, in any case, a photocopy was not an official document. Every time I was out and about now I imagined myself getting stopped by a policeman or a soldier who was unimpressed by my piece of paper. If it had been some time since he'd nabbed an illegal immigrant he would be itching to make an arrest. And, this is where I come in. Dragged off to the local nick, shoved into a cell, protesting my innocence to deaf ears. And how long would I be left to vegetate before somebody got round to checking me out. No way. I have to have my passport, and I can't wait two months. I want my passport, and I want it now.

Later that day Sally and I popped into Kuwait City. She had a parcel to post. After the post office we went walkabout. However, very soon, the sun started to get to us. This made the shadowy interior of a KFC irresistibly attractive. We went in. We opted for ice cream.

'How was it for you?' I asked Sally, as she pushed her empty tub to one side.

'Perfect,' she replied.

I had resolved not to raise the topic of my passport and had successfully done this thus far, until I dropped my guard. And, before I could stop it, my passport gripe had elbowed its way into the conversation. I told Sally about my conversation with Joanna that morning. With a false chuckle, I asked Sally if she knew a good safecracker. She laughed.

'What on earth for?' she asked. 'Are you planning to rob a bank?'

'No, of course not. I don't even want to steal anything. I just want back what's mine, my passport. But while it's in David's safe it might as well be on the moon.'

'But getting it back might not be that difficult.'

'What do you mean?'

'Well, you cause a kerfuffle in the foyer and David rushes out to see what's going on. Then, while everybody is focused on the commotion, you nip in, grab your passport and nip back out again.'

'I don't understand the 'just open the safe door' bit,' I said.

'Well, when I was in David's office getting my passport just a couple of months ago he simply opened the safe, pulled out the pile of passports and then merely pushed the door over. I would imagine his safe is open all day. After all, there is no real reason for it to be locked while he is in the office.

'A dashed clever plan – but there is a snag. There is no way I could ever muster the nerve to start a to-do in the foyer.'

'Well, you weren't really serious about trying to extricate your passport from David's safe, were you?'

'No, of course I wasn't.' At this we both laughed.

I tried to get some work done at my desk that evening but my attempt was less than half-hearted. What ingenious chain of events would lead to my standing in front of the safe in David's office on my own? Would I have the bottle to take the first step?

Next day, after lunch, I asked George if he fancied a little trip to the Sultan Centre. He did. I did not let on that the attraction of the Sultan Centre was the possibility of seeing Joanna there. Had I done so he wouldn't have come with me. So, instead, I went on a bit about the quality of the Centre's fruit and vegetables. I could have gone by myself but I had come to dislike going about on my own. I said I would phone for the taxi. I think for some childish reason I wanted to be the one who christened our phone. As ever, it was the big white Ford that came for us. By now we were very friendly and chatty with Anwar. In the supermarket, I pushed my trolley at a very slow browsing speed. George angrily disapproved of this arthritic snail's pace at which I was going and, unable to keep down with this painfully slow rate of progress, went upstairs for a coffee. After completing three or four tours of the shop floor, I reluctantly headed for the checkout. I left the supermarket feeling disappointed. I could have done with seeing Joanna that day. I was confused and discontented. Things were getting worse. And, there was something about Joanna that helped. Now, chatting with Joanna seemed to be the only thing that did. But there never seemed to be enough time at the College. I could simply have asked Joanna out for dinner, but I feared that my motives might be misconstrued. If it started to look to Joanna like I fancied my chances she would probably see me in a different light, and she wouldn't like what she saw. I'm bound to bump into her here another day, I told myself. Outside the Centre, assuming that George was still inside, I waited. However, before George came out my patiencc ran out, so I gave up and took a taxi home.

When I got back to the flat George was already in residence. What a shoot-through, I thought. George looked up, said hello, and went straight back into his book.

That evening while I was watching the news my mind kept returning to the conversation I'd had with Sally. Was extricating my passport a viable proposition? I felt sure I could come up with some sort of plan, but no matter how good this was it would still be a risky business. Something always goes wrong in those sort of situations. I wondered what the College would do if I were caught. If they decided not to press criminal charges they would probably just sack me and send me home. If they decided to prosecute me and call the police, I would end up in a Kuwaiti clink. Armed guards, a rock-hard bed and a nightmare number of creepy-crawlies as cellmates. And cuisine a million miles away from haute. And how long would I be left to rot there? I reasoned that the critical question in all this concerned the reason why the College was holding my passport in the first place. Was it really that they did not want to ruffle the feathers of Immigration by not having everybody's passport immediately available when they called for them? Or, was the College holding my passport as a means of holding me? Was I in effect being held captive? And how long would this go on? Six months? A year? And what would this detention be all about? Was the College a front for something? Would somebody approach me in a few months time with an ultimatum? Do this for us or you never get back home. I decided I would have to risk getting caught in the act. I had to get my passport back. If the safe was open, then the entire operation would only take a few seconds. Would the safe be unlocked? I thought about David's behaviour. I knew he popped up to the staff room during both the morning and the evening breaks to make a coffee. Did he lock his office? On more than one occasion, while I was working in the library, I had seen David leave his office to go upstairs and I had no recollection of seeing him locking his office door. He would emerge, pull his door behind him, disappear upstairs, return a few minutes later with his coffee, turn the handle of his door and go straight in. I don't ever remember seeing him fumbling with keys. Could I nip in and out of David's office while he was upstairs, without being noticed?

The following evening I didn't go to my Arabic class. I told George I wasn't feeling well. I went over to the College just before eight, and sat in the foyer. At exactly eight o'clock David came out of his office and went upstairs. He did not lock his office door. The passport recovery mission was possible. The foyer was choc-a- bloc with students. At the mid-evening break it probably always was. I felt it was reasonable to believe that I could enter and leave David's office without being noticed by Ebtisan at reception. All I needed was the bottle to do it. Throughout the next day I argued with myself. Be brave, I told myself, go for it. Don't be a fool, it's not worth the risk. That evening, I again said to George that I wasn't feeling well and that I would not be going to our evening class.

I entered the college at about quarter to eight. I sat in the foyer. As usual at this time, it was full of students. As it approached eight o'clock I got up and, feeling slightly weightless I drifted over to a notice board right next to the door of David's office. I pretended to be reading the notices. At exactly eight o'clock David suddenly came out of his office. And, in the blink of an eye, he had gone. I looked round. Ebtisan was surrounded by umpteen students. I moved nearer the office door. By the time I was reaching for the door handle my mouth was bone dry, my tongue felt as thick as a boot heel and generally I felt as weak as a sickly kitten. I stepped inside, pushed the door behind me and went straight to the safe. It was perched on a bench immediately behind David's desk. I grasped the door handle. I hesitated for a second. I pulled. The door opened. There was a pile of passports on the bottom shelf at the front. I lifted them out and started to remove the elastic band that was holding them together. Suddenly, the pile seemed to jump into the air and landed all over the floor. I frantically started to pick them up. While I was doing so, there it was, my passport. What a beautiful passport it is, I said to myself. I stuffed my passport into my hip pocket and put the remainder back into the safe. Just as I was closing the safe I heard voices just outside the office door. It sounded like David. I looked round. There was a door. I leapt towards it. It was unlocked. I slipped inside, and closed it behind me. It was a stationery store. The light was already on. I squeezed myself in between the far wall and the storage shelves. I could faintly hear voices in the office. I crouched down. I guessed I was going to be here for some time. I dozed and woke for at least a couple of hours. At this point, I went and stood and listened behind the storeroom door. All seemed quiet. Thankfully, the door was still unlocked. I eased it open. The office was in darkness. I looked around. I could see the dark shadow of a lamp on David's desk. I switched it on. I didn't expect the office door to be unlocked but I checked it anyway. Locked it was. How do I get out of here, I wondered. The window in David's office was a large solid panel of glass bricks. The only direct access to the outside world was a small flap-door that had been fitted instead of a brick. I soon resigned myself to the idea that I was here for the night. I realised it would probably be the mid-morning break before I would get a chance to escape. Before David's arrival in the morning I would have to return to the stationery store. I sank myself into David's large, black, swivelly chair. I don't remember sitting for long in the hours of darkness. When I awoke, day was beginning to break. I felt slightly uncomfortable. Oh no, I said to myself, nature's calling. Trouble is, how the hell do I answer it? I scanned the office. David's waste paper bin was metal, but full of paper. A possibility, I said to myself. I eventually decided that it would have to be the small door in the window. However, this was at chest height. There were several side chairs in the room. I dragged one across to the window to stand on. Perfect. On my return to

David's desk, I immediately found myself snooping around. There was little on the desk. I caught sight of a note pad. On the first page inside there was a memo which read:

Fax *to No. 1.*

Latest two seem ideal. Few fam ties. Min com with UK. Both attending Arabic classes and seem keen.
David

That seems to be about George and me, I said to myself. What does it mean?

Suddenly I heard a jangle of keys at the office door. It was the cleaner. I realised that this was my chance to get out. So, I made no effort to hide. I sat tight and tried to look unconcerned.

'Good morning, Mina,' I said.

'Good morning, Mr Jack,' she replied, approaching the desk.

She picked up the waste paper bin and emptied its contents into the black bin liner she had been dragging.

'Oh well,' I said, getting to my feet, 'I think I've done enough. Time I was getting home for a bit of shut eye.'

As I made my way slowly to the office door, Mina casually said, ' Bye, Mr Jack.'

I half walked and half jogged out of the College and back to the flat. I gently eased open the door of the flat and crept inside. I literally tip-toed to my bedroom and, as quietly as I could, closed the door behind me. I sat on the edge of my bed and automatically sighed hugely. I pulled my passport from my pocket. Just holding it made me feel good. I felt free. Free at last, I said to myself.

Chapter Six

As summer approached, the increase in the heat of the sun became a significant aspect of everyday life. Just how to keep cool during the day became a more and more important consideration. The air-conditioning in the flat was now on permanently. The reason for the siesta tradition became obvious. Many shops remained open in the afternoons but fewer and fewer people ventured out to go to them. Like a mad dog I continued to go out every day and by early summer I was popping down to Salyma every other afternoon. This was entirely due to my finding the chance of meeting Joanna in the Sultan Centre irresistible, since she invariably invited me round to her flat. Joanna must have known that my bumping into her so frequently was not accidental, but she didn't seem to mind. The trip to Salyma was made entirely bearable and quite comfortable by the highly efficient air conditioning system in Anwar's cab. Anwar eventually started acting like my personal chauffer on these afternoons. Rather than shoot away after dropping me off at the Centre, he would wait until I had completed my shopping. If I re-emerged alone, knowing that this meant I would be needing an immediate lift back to Dasmah, he would appear and lead me to his car. If I came out with Joanna he would not approach me. But he would be sitting waiting for me when a few hours later I came out of Joanna's flat. By this time I was well convinced that Anwar was keeping a spying eye on me.

I was glad to be teaching, but I was doing much too little. George too complained that he wasn't doing nearly enough. We decided to take up a sport that we could do in our free time. An outdoor activity was out because of the blistering heat. The International Hotel had a sports club but both George and I hated gymnasiums, and the annual fee was so high that it would not have been worth joining simply to use the swimming pool. George discovered a young men's club and without much hesitation, this we joined. It had ten-pin bowling, table tennis, snooker and pool. After a brief spell of trial and error we found that our game was pool.

One day, in Joanna's flat, fate ran amok with my emotions. If I didn't understand it before, I certainly fully understood after that day the full meaning of the concept of dilemma. As soon as I said it was getting close to my time to leave, Joanna asked me if I would like to stay to dinner. It was a beautiful shock and surprise and it rendered me speechless. I had arranged to go out with Sally that evening. I played for time by coughing and clearing my throat, as my mind raced about desperately seeking a suitable response. I stole a bit of time by thanking

Joanna and saying it would be wonderful. Failing to find anything better to say, I practically begged Joanna to let me have a rain check on her invitation. She said she would of course and added that she was just sorry I couldn't make it that evening. I spent most of my journey home in a sort of trance, stunned and silenced by disbelief. I couldn't believe my misfortune. An invitation I would have given any number of right arms for, and when it happens I am unable to accept it. Having arranged to go out with Sally, there was just no way at this late hour that I could cancel. I didn't really want to anyway. I was looking forward to our date. Trouble is, although Joanna said she didn't mind, I felt certain that she would interpret my declining her invitation as a rebuff. She would never ask me again. I could feel a few days of grovelling and sucking up coming up. Somehow I had to re-ingratiate myself with Joanna. I was already painfully aware how difficult, if not impossible, this would be. Things between Joanna and me had been going wonderfully well. Her inviting me back to her flat must have meant she at least enjoyed my company. And today's dinner invitation surely confirmed that. Have I ruined everything?

I was left hanging on tenterhooks for two days before I met Joanna again. I was making myself a coffee in the staff room when somebody came and stood by my side. It was Joanna. 'Hi,' she said brightly. I tried hard to think of something clever and poignant to say, but couldn't. What came out was: 'Can I make you a coffee?'

'Oh, yes please,' she replied. We sat and chatted for a good ten minutes before she had to get back to work. It was as if two days ago had never happened.

I'd detected a gradual change in George's demeanour. Going and almost gone were his usual self-assuredness and characteristic alacrity. Apart from the odd night of pool, he was spending his evenings in the flat. It seemed he'd had a bust up with Liz. I kept asking him if everything was okay. He invariably responded by simply saying he was fine.

I could always sense when George was in the flat, even when I could not hear him or knew for certain that he was in. One morning, as I was making a coffee, I knew for certain that George was not in the flat. I told myself that he probably got up and went out early for some reason. Later that day, Joanna came to the flat. It was the first time that she had done so. Something was wrong. She asked me if I had seen George or heard anything from him. I said I hadn't. She said George hadn't turned up for his forenoon class. Joanna asked me to let her know if and when I saw George or if he made contact with me. I said of course I would. After a couple of days of no George, I was certain that he was not going to come back. Without his passport he could not have left the country. He had to still be in Kuwait. Maybe he was hiding somewhere. Perhaps he felt he had to get away for some reason. Time to think or just chill out. Maybe he had been arrested. A chill ran down my spine and I felt my scalp tingle. Suddenly, I seemed to know what George's disappearance was all about. He had been abducted.

I decided to pay Nigel a visit. The College management's apparent indifference about George's disappearance was starting to get to me. They seemed to be making no attempt to find out what had happened to him. There had to be something they could do. I knocked Nigel's office door and went straight in. He was sitting behind his big empty desk reading *The Times* and drinking coffee. As he folded his paper and laid it on the desk, he wished me good morning and asked me what he could do for me. I asked him if he had any news about George. He said he was afraid he had not. I asked him if he had reported George as a missing person to the police.

'I doubt whether the police would be interested,' he said. I put it to Nigel that this was rather negative thinking. 'Well,' he said, 'we tend to lose teachers, especially males, and the police have always maintained that there was nothing they could do about it.'

'But surely there is something you can do?'

‘Actually, Jack, I think you are worrying unnecessarily about your friend. He’s probably back in Old Blighty, safe and well.’

‘But he can’t be,’ I said. ‘He couldn’t have left Kuwait. He didn’t have his passport.’

‘Ah, well, that’s not exactly true,’ said Nigel.

‘What do you mean?’

‘George demanded the return of his passport shortly after handing it over on day one, and David and I felt we had little choice but to agree to this.’

‘But he would have told me,’ I said firmly.

‘We explained to George that we could only make such a concession on one condition. He would have to keep the fact that he had been allowed to hold onto his passport a secret. He agreed to this.’

I didn’t linger in Nigel’s office. I wasn’t at all happy with his response to my concerns. Later, in class, I gave such a poor presentation I felt I ought to apologise to my students at the end of the lesson.

Back at the flat I couldn’t think of anything to do. I leaned on the window ledge and gazed out of the window. I was unhappy and confused. My spirits were raised by a visit from Joanna. She asked me if there was anything she could do. I told her about Nigel’s assertion that George had been allowed to keep his passport, and that I doubted whether this could have been the case. She said she would try to find out the truth. Before she left she asked me what I was doing after my Arabic class in the evening. It crossed my mind to try to make some joke about the possibility of my going clubbing, but thankfully I desisted, and said I was doing nothing in particular. She told me not to eat before my class and that she would be along later to cook a meal for me with a surprise.

Joanna arrived at the flat shortly after nine carrying a full poly bag of shopping. She went straight to the kitchen. I slouched at the kitchen door while she unpacked her bag. Suddenly she stopped and looked straight at me with a mischievous smile on her face. Then, like a magician performing a conjuring trick, she produced from her bag a bottle of wine.

'Now, that can't be real,' I said.

'Homemade,' she replied, 'but real wine none the less. And not a bad drop of stuff, even though I say so myself. Do you have glasses?'

'I'm afraid I haven't,' I said.

'Mugs it is then,' she said.

Joanna made probably the best risotto I had ever had, and the wine added the finishing touch to what was altogether a wonderful meal. We dined by the light of a lamp on the coffee table; this was Joanna's idea. It wasn't quite candlelight or the glow of a log fire but it nevertheless helped to create the sort of after-dinner ambiance that followed the saturation of the senses and led to a dreamy state in which it was impossible for a man to forget for a moment the essential difference between himself and the woman opposite. Just before midnight Joanna said it was time she hit the road. As she stood up to leave, I thanked her and said, 'It was a wonderful meal and a wonderful evening.'

'Oh, thanks for having me,' she said. 'I've had a lovely evening.'

'I'll come down with you to the car.'

'Not at all,' she replied, 'I'll be perfectly safe.'

As we said good night Joanna hesitated for several seconds before turning away.

In class the following morning, thankfully, I did a better job for my students than I had done the day before. Later, when Joanna came into the staff room, I went over to her. I asked her if she had any news about George.

'None at all, I'm afraid,' she said.

'Did you get a chance to ask Nigel about the passport?'

'Yes,' she said, 'but he merely repeated the story he'd told you the other day. Apparently, George said he'd turn round and go straight back home rather than hand over his passport. Nigel said he felt he had no option but to try to get an assurance from George that he would tell absolutely nobody that the College had allowed him to retain his passport.'

First thing that afternoon I popped down to Sally's. She welcomed me in but immediately asked me if I would mind her continuing with her packing.

'Packing?'

'Yes,' she said, 'I'm off back home tonight. I've had my flight booked since last week. Didn't I tell you?'

'No.'

'Oh, I am sorry, Jack,' she said, 'I really do have a dreadful memory.'

I asked Sally when she was leaving. She said her taxi would be along in about an hour. I asked her if she would like me to stay to help her with her case. 'Not at all,' she said, 'I'll manage okay.' I wished Sally safe journey and a great holiday. She threw her arms around me and hugged me tightly. I left Sally's flat and climbed the stairs with a lump in my throat. In the flat, I stood in the middle of the living room floor feeling rather stunned and confused. That was all I needed… losing Sally. What next? Do something, I said to myself. That's the answer. Do something worthwhile. Achieve something. My mental search stopped at food. I thought about curries. I loved curries but I'd never made one that was anything more than a vague reminder of the delicious dish that Indian restaurants make. I recalled a celebrity chef in the UK stating that the secret of all successful cooking was passion. That's what I'll do. I won't simply cook a curry, I'll create one with tender loving care. I couldn't wait. I went straight into the kitchen and got out all the ingredients I would need. I placed them on the worktop. I measured and mixed my spices with fine precision. I chopped, sliced and grated with loving care and laid everything into the pan. Don't stir. Gently give the ingredients a tour of the pan. Don't leave. Stay and watch over that magical transformation as individual delights blend and become a marvellous *melange*. Looks good, I said to myself. It smells good. Is it ready? Yes it is. I carefully poured the heady golden mixture onto a bed of basmati rice. With optimistic anticipation I carried my creation ceremoniously through to the dining table. I think I've done it, I said to myself as I sat in. Slide the fork in. Into the mouth. Yes? No. Usual rubbish. Undaunted, I strode back into the kitchen, determined to make a success of something. I carefully considered the gastronomic delights and experiences that were promised by each of a range of different dishes. I settled for sardines on toast.

I could have done with work to go to the following morning, but it was the first day of the weekend. After breakfast, I sat looking around and wondering what to do. It was spookily quiet. Even George's radio cassette, still sitting on the coffee table, seemed eerily silent. I wonder where he is right now? I hope he is okay, wherever he is. Doubts and thoughts began to flood into my mind. Could he have been abducted? The College couldn't really be a front for something, could it? I was sure Nigel had lied about George's passport, but this left the question of why. And who or what was Anwar? And why was the *harres* always snooping around? I had been sitting thinking for more than an hour when there was a knock at the door. It was Joanna. She said she had popped up to see if I fancied going for a swim at the hotel. Without hesitation I said I didn't. She asked me how I was getting on. I didn't reply. Instead I found I couldn't resist this opportunity to ask her again about George's passport, and whether Nigel was being honest about it. She said she believed Nigel, and couldn't think of any reason why he would lie. I suddenly found myself asking Joanna if she knew that the College had a print room that had been sealed off. She simply said, no. Wrong answer, Joanna, I said to myself.

Joanna asked me if I was sure I didn't want to go for a swim. I said I was sure. Shortly after that she left. So, even Joanna's lying to me. What's going on at that College? What the hell could it be? Why would they want two English blokes in Kuwait? But not any two blokes. They want two teachers. In other words, two fairly intelligent blokes. Maybe the two guys that we replaced are in on this too. So, maybe they need four altogether and, according to David's fax note, not having much communication with the UK is also important. The Arabic language and culture class is probably part of it too. They probably want us to become fluent in Arabic. Why would somebody in Kuwait want four British guys fluent in Arabic and with no strong UK ties? And who would want them? It has to be the CIA, it couldn't be anybody else. They're famous for their secret missions. They must have a job for us to do. A mission. Why in Kuwait? Kuwait has just been in a war, it must have something to do with that. Suddenly, it all became terrifyingly clear to me. George has been taken into a brainwashing phase. In some secret location somewhere, here in Kuwait, possibly with two other blokes, George is going through mind alteration. I'm next. I've got to get out of here. I've got my passport. So, now, plan B. The escape plan.

I couldn't think. I went through to my bedroom and lay down. The phone rang. It was the first time it had rung. I didn't know anybody had our number. I dashed through to the living room and answered the phone. It was Joanna. She told me to have some half-decent gear on by seven. 'We are going out for a curry' she said. I told her firmly I wasn't in a going-out mood.

'By the way,' I said, 'how did you know my number?' She said she had seen it this afternoon and had taken a mental note of it. She asked me again about going out this evening. Again I said no. There was a short silence. Joanna then said:

'Okay', and put the phone down.

I tried to think of the point this afternoon at which Joanna looked at my phone. I couldn't remember it. Once more, I went into my thinking and analysing mode.

At just after seven, while I was tucking into beans on toast, the door opened and in walked Joanna. She was carrying two bottles of wine. She plonked them on the dining table, went through to the kitchen, came back with two mugs, filled them up and placed one in front of me. She sat opposite.

'Okay', she said, 'what's up?'

'Nothing'.

'No, not nothing,' she said, 'something. Something is bugging you. What is it?' I discovered I was still going through one of those rather inconvenient honesty phases.

'I can't believe you don't know about the print room. You're covering up something. That's what's bugging me.'

'Okay, Jack, I'll admit to knowing about the print room but I can't tell you any more than that. I assure you there is nothing sinister about it. It's all quite innocent. The College has to try to keep the existence of the print room secret. I am virtually on oath about this. I can't tell anybody about it, even you. Please trust me. Anyway, there's no reason at all why any of the teaching staff need be worried about the existence of the print room. Please believe me.'

Joanna is telling the truth. Suddenly, I had no doubts about that.

'I believe you', I said. 'But I'm still not a happy man. There are other things, very worrying things.'

'What sort of things?'

'Well, would you believe it's my turn to say I can't tell you. There is something going on at the College that you obviously know nothing about. If I told you, it would simply have you worried. You're not in any danger. I am. I am now going to tell you something but it has to be strictly between you and me'.

'Of course', Joanna said.

'While I still can, I've got to get away from here. I've got to leave Kuwait.'

'But, are you absolutely sure you're in that sort of danger here?'

'Very sure', I said.

'This is dreadful news, Jack, but of course, I will not say a word about it to a soul. Is there anything at all I can do to help? I want to help. How will you get out of Kuwait?'

'Well, the obvious way is to fly out. But for precisely that reason, I'll have to go some other way. The people who do not want me to leave Kuwait will have people at the airport right now, just waiting to apprehend me if I were silly enough to try to fly out. So, my plan is to hire a car and drive down through Saudi to Bahrain. They would never believe that I would have the audacity to try to pull off a little stunt like that.'

'But you can't hire a car, Jack. You've got to have residency before you can hire a car. Also, you would never get a visa and the bundle of assorted permits you would need to drive through Saudi. You would need your residency for that too. And what about your passport? You haven't even got that'.

'Yes, I have.'

'Oh.'

'Don't ask.'

'Jack, please, please trust me. You're clearly not a happy man, and I would like to help. But I can't even begin to help until I know exactly what is going on in that troubled mind of yours.' My mind searched at the gallop for a suitable response. I did trust Joanna, but I seemed to know that if there was just the slightest crack in the absolute secrecy surrounding the way I got my passport back, I'd be a nervous wreck, constantly waiting for a heavy hand to clamp onto my shoulder. I promised Joanna that I would tell all soon.

'I'll get a ship. I'll sail away.'

'But passenger ships don't come into Kuwait.'

'Okay, I'll stow away on a cargo ship.'

'But it's a secure dockyard. You would never get into the dock or near a ship without the right papers. And, there are no trains in Kuwait. Furthermore, the bus service is an entirely domestic one. There's only one way out of Kuwait.' Joanna's face lit up. She was obviously struggling to hold back laughter. 'Of course, if you were up to it, you could always walk several hundred miles across the desert and make your escape by swimming across the Red Sea.'

'No, I'll steal a rowing boat from somewhere and row across the Gulf'.

'Into Iran? Not recommended.'

'Okay, the airport it is. I'll just have to think of a way to get through unnoticed '

Joanna left just after midnight. I sat thinking for a while, sipping the last of my wine. I wondered if I had done the right thing in telling Joanna about my escape plans. Yes, I told myself. She would probably prove to be a valuable friend. There was something about Joanna that made me trust her.

Chapter Seven

'Have you devised your ingenious new plan yet?' asked Joanna.

'Why do you ask?'

'Oh, no, you're not still suspecting me of being one of the baddies, are you, for goodness sake?'

'No, of course I'm not.'

'I'm sorry and, yes, I have come up with a new plan, but I can't tell you what it is yet. Plenty of time for that.'

'You still haven't told me what the danger you have to escape from is.'

'You'll find out someday. I don't want to trouble you with that just now.'

'Right', said Joanna, 'I'm off. I'll be back at eight. Be ready.' The audacity department of my mind dared me with a mischievous and undoubtedly risky offer of "okay boss" as an appropriate response to Joanna's assertiveness, but I yielded not and opted for that traditional and highly successful keeper of the peace:

'Yes, dear.'

I felt I had swithered and dithered long enough about when and how I would effect my escape from Kuwait. I'll go soon. There is a KLM flight at one in the morning. Arranging everything at the very last minute was surely the best plan. I decided it would be best to leave the flat during the hours of darkness, but I would still need a disguise. Anwar would immediately radio in and raise the alarm about my escape bid. I would get Joanna to buy my ticket from the KLM office in Kuwait City in the afternoon. At the same time, she could buy me some traditional Kuwaiti clothing. Just buying an airline ticket would be risky, but it was a risk I would have to take. There was no other way out of Kuwait. Also in the afternoon, tomorrow, I would pop into the Gulf Bank and close my account. Leaving this to the very last minute was also a good idea, I had reasoned. Somebody at the bank could contact the College.

In the Maharajah that evening I gave Joanna the details of my plan. I got Joanna to repeat everything. She convinced me that she was all about on my plan. As soon as she had done so she pulled me up for bolting my food. In mitigation I said I was probably suffering a slight loss of my memory of social and cultural norms due to a little light-headedness probably brought on by my having survived for the past week on scrambled egg or beans on toast. 'Rubbish,' said Joanna firmly, 'there's no such thing as an excuse for acting like a pig in public.' Here we go again, I said to myself.

'Yes, dear,' I said.

Later, outside my flat, before I got out of Joanna's car, I quite spontaneously leaned over and kissed her on the cheek.

It felt really weird going to work in a College that I now knew had, under the guise of taking me on as a teacher, in fact quite ruthlessly recruited me to take part in some sort of mission. I presented my class with all the flair and teaching skills of a robot who had bluffed his way into the profession. Later, when I had just made a coffee in the staff room, Joanna came in. Thanking me, she lifted the cup and told me to make one for myself. She told me to have a look at the staff notice board. Among the assorted bits of paper that had been on the board for several weeks, there was one fresh-looking sheet of paper. It was signed by David. It stated that in view of the continuing clampdown by the government on illegal immigration, passports currently being held for the purposes of residency application would be immediately returned. I made another coffee and joined Joanna at my desk.

'Does that give you problems?' asked Joanna.

'Possibly. If I don't go and ask for my passport and David notices this, he might get suspicious. He'll at least be puzzled and want to ask me about it. And, if he concludes that I must have somehow retrieved it, he'll tell Nigel and they'll know that I'd smelled a rat. And, that I probably had doing a runner in mind.'

'What are you going to do?' asked Joanna.

'Well, that's it, I've got to go as soon as possible. Tonight.'

'But, doesn't that notice indicate that the College isn't keeping your passport just to stop you leaving Kuwait?' asked Joanna.

'I can't take that chance. This little move could be designed to lull me into the proverbial false sense of security.'

I took what I knew would be my last class. At the end of the lesson I said goodbye rather than cheerio to my students, knowing that they wouldn't suss the significance of this. I had arranged to meet Joanna outside the Gulf Bank at two. But, shortly after midday she appeared at the flat. She said she wanted to avoid being seen hanging about outside the bank on her own. Good thinking, I said to myself. Joanna had left her car at the College and suggested that we walk into the City. This was another good idea. It would give us a chance to chat and finalise details of my plan. We parted at the steps of the bank. I went inside. Joanna went to do a bit of window-shopping. As ever, the bank was full. After an exasperating half hour wait I got to the front of the queue. When I asked about closing my account the teller directed me to another window.

Thankfully, here there was only a queue of two. While I was waiting, I spotted one of my students, Fahti, at a desk behind the tellers. When I got to the front of the queue he came over to the window and asked me if I was being attended to. I said I was and that my teller had simply slipped away for a moment. Had they even placed a spy amongst my students? The teller gave me the balance of my account, six hundred and fifty pounds in fifty-pound notes. I gathered the notes and turned away. As I was stuffing my money into my wallet a voice said, 'Hello there, Jack'. It was Nigel. 'Going on a bit of a spending spree?' he asked.

'Yes, just plushing up the flat a bit,' I said. I didn't hang about. I was only half way down the steps of the bank when Joanna came along. Brilliant, I thought to myself. Perfect timing. I gave Joanna some money and asked her to get my plane ticket and the clothes I needed.

I went straight back to the flat. About two hours later Joanna came in. Before I could ask she said, 'Got everything.' She placed one poly bag on George's chair, told me to sit where I was at the dining table, and disappeared into the kitchen with another poly bag. In next to no time she emerged with two heaped plates of something. I didn't know what it was, and didn't ask, but it was delicious.

Joanna clearly wanted to test my resolve. 'Jack,' she said, 'even at this late hour you can change your mind. Are you absolutely sure you want to go through with your escape? Are you sure your suspicions are correct?'

'Yes, I'm very sure. Nigel follows me into the bank and you still have doubts? Nigel already had me sussed and Fahti would have confirmed this by telling him that I had closed my account. There's probably somebody across the street right now guarding the flats. I probably won't be allowed to get into a taxi tonight.'

'But your meeting Nigel at the bank was probably a complete coincidence,' said Joanna.

'Wrong. Too much of a coincidence.'

'Jack, darling, I'm beginning to feel very nervous about all this.' Snap, I said to myself. 'Please, you must tell me the nature of the danger you feel you are in,' said Joanna.

I felt compelled to try to allay Joanna's fears. I had no choice but to fully confide in her.

'I have been recruited to join a hit squad and carry out an assassination.'

Joanna's mouth dropped. 'You've what?' she exclaimed.

'Right now, at some location, probably the College's Hawalli site, George and others are going through a brain-washing program. Nigel's next task is to get me to join them.'

'Brainwashed?' asked Joanna. 'Assassinate? Who?'

'Saddam, of course.'
'How could you possibly know that?'
'It was in the news on the telly just the other day. Apparently some American hard-liners are saying that their forces didn't finish the job, and that they should have gone on into Baghdad and either arrested or bumped off Saddam. They suggested that a small assassination squad would now be the best way of getting rid of the Iraqi leader.'
'But that's a million miles away from you and George being taken on by the College as teachers.'
'Is it?'
Joanna said she would have to show her face at the College. She hugged me and told me she would be back in a couple of hours. What do I do now? I asked myself. I still haven't done any packing. I had decided to travel light. I stuffed some clothing and lots of items I decided I either wanted or needed into a travel bag. Now, time to get dressed. Putting on the *dishdasha* was quite straightforward. The *ghatra* was a bit more difficult. When I got it looking roughly right, I secured it with the *agal*. This immediately improved the look of the thing. Well, it will have to do. My ticket, where's my ticket? I searched but couldn't find it. Joanna must still have it.
When Joanna returned I was sitting at my desk in my bedroom. To complete my disguise I put on my sunglasses and went through to the living room.

Joanna was wearing a long skirt and carrying a shoulder bag. She also had a case. I was wondering about her attire but was distracted by her laughter. 'What's so funny?' I asked.

'Your head gear isn't on right,' she replied.

'Okay then, smarty-pants, you sort it.'

'I don't really know how a *ghatra* is put on, I just know yours is not right.'

'Oh well, it will have to do,' I said. 'My airline ticket, you forgot to leave it.'

'No, I didn't,' Joanna said. 'I didn't have it earlier, but I do have it now.' I wondered what she meant by this, but I didn't ask. I reasoned that the answer would probably confuse me as much the statement did. My attention returned to Joanna's long skirt and her case. But, before I got time to ask, clearly reading what the expression on my face was telling her about what was in my mind, Joanna said:

'The case?'

'Yes, why the case and why the long skirt?'

'I'm coming with you.'

Chapter Eight

'You can't,' I said loudly, more in disbelief than in anger.

'Why not?'

'I don't know' was the best I could come up with as a quick response. 'What about your car and your flat?' I asked.

'I've left both sets of keys in Liz's mailbox, with a note, I'll write to her later.'

'An airline ticket, you haven't got a ticket.'

'Yes I have, I bought one when I was getting yours. Now, not another word. Get on the phone and book a taxi.'

Completely stuck for words, I moved close to Joanna and hugged her. This lasted for several minutes.

As our watches crept towards eleven I became increasingly nervy. I was now glad Joanna was coming with me. Everything she did and said was helpful. After a long spell of thinking and talking everything through, and making sure we had everything we needed, we decided to go downstairs to wait for the taxi. Before leaving the flat Joanna covered her head with a scarf and I put on my sunglasses. I looked in the mirror. Brilliant. My own mother wouldn't know me. We made our way downstairs. Thankfully, the *Harres's* door was closed. While we were waiting in the foyer, I remembered Joanna telling me that she hadn't bought my airline ticket right away after our visit to the bank. I quizzed her about this. She explained that she was on her way to the KLM office when she suddenly felt she ought to try once more to change my mind about running from Kuwait.

'When I got here, I very soon discovered that there was no way you would change your mind,' she said. 'It was at that point that I decided to go with you. So, when I left you, I popped back into the KLM office and bought our tickets.'

At exactly eleven o'clock a taxi drew up outside the flats. As soon as we stepped out of the flats, the driver got out and went to the back of the car.

'Hello, Mr. Jack,' he said.

'Who are you?' I asked. He said his name was Abdul and that he had come to take us to the airport. I glanced towards Joanna. She shrugged her shoulders. I wondered why it wasn't Anwar that had come for us. Of course, I said to myself, the CIA have told Anwar to let them know if and when I make an unusual move. My requesting a cab so late in the evening has made Anwar suspicious. That's why he's stayed in the office. As soon as Abdul radios in his destination, Anwar will get straight onto the phone. Despite my having sussed what was going on, I decided we had little choice but to act cool and carry on regardless. Abdul put our cases in the boot and we got into the back seat. As soon as we were on the move, Abdul lifted his radio handset and said something to his control. Joanna leaned towards me and whispered that he had told them he was on his way to the airport. This is what I had expected to happen. They now knew I was making my bid to escape. What we did at the airport now depended on what Abdul did. I could grab my own bag, but if Abdul insisted on carrying Joanna's case, I would have to split. Abdul's being with us inside the terminal would immediately blow my cover. I would then not be able to escape. There would be several guns pointing towards me. My only chance would be to make a run for it outside the terminal and indicate to Joanna to stay in the taxi and then simply return home. Nobody was after her. She would be okay.

Soon after we had set off, Abdul turned left. This to my reckoning was in a southerly direction. We eventually came to a junction on Cairo Road. Here, again, Abdul turned left, and south. I didn't know the route to the airport well, but I felt sure that at that junction he should have gone straight across and headed west. I glanced towards Joanna but she seemed unconcerned. I asked Abdul if he was on the right road for the airport. He said, 'Yes, we go to airport.' I still didn't like it and was becoming increasingly concerned. It seemed to me that we were heading for Hawalli, a densely populated suburb.

Suddenly, Abdul turned the car hard to the right. We bumped over the kerb and onto a large area of spare ground. This took us into semi darkness. I didn't know what to say or do. I thought perhaps Abdul was having trouble with his car. When we were about a hundred yards from the main road, Abdul stopped the car. I asked him if everything was okay. He swung round. He had a pistol. He pointed it straight at me. 'Your money, Mr. Jack,' he said. I didn't stop to think. I lunged forward and grabbed his wrists. I managed to twist his hand so that the pistol was pointing upwards. It was now a test of strength. Suddenly, Joanna's hand shot forward and wrenched the gun from Abdul's grasp. She immediately held the pistol at Abdul's temple and yelled something in Arabic. I could feel Abdul's strength melting away. Joanna handed the pistol to me and told me to hold it close to Abdul's head. She got out and went round to the back of the car. A few seconds later she returned with a pair of tights in her hand. She again said something to Abdul. He put his hands behind his back, and Joanna swiftly tied his wrists together.

'Okay, boss, what do we do now?' she asked me.

'I think we'd better get out of here. When Abdul doesn't report his arrival at the airport, I suspect another car will be out here soon. Right, let's go.' I laid the pistol on the back seat. Joanna and I got out of the car. As I was getting out, I caught my *ghatra* at the top of the door frame, and it fell onto the back seat. I just left it there. Joanna and I lifted out our luggage.

We headed off into the darkness. 'Where are we heading for?' Joanna asked.

'I haven't a clue,' I replied. 'I think the best idea would be to find somewhere that we could hide, possibly a place where we could spend the night.'

'Why don't we just get to a main road, hail a taxi and carry on to the airport?' asked Joanna.

'Well, as you well know, Kuwaiti taxis are not supposed to pick up fares, we could wait for hours, and on a main road a bad idea when there is bound to be at least one car cruising around looking for us. Anyway, they're still waiting for me to show at the airport. My disguise has been blown. If I were to step into the terminal they would immediately pounce on me.'

The number of flats and houses, on the edge of what was proving to be a huge empty area gradually increased. Ahead, through the darkness, I could see an apartment block, standing alone, that seemed to be empty. As we got nearer, I could see there were no lights on anywhere in the building. It seemed to be an abandoned block. We walked right round, checking the windows to confirm that there were no lights on. 'I think we've landed lucky,' I said. We crept slowly towards the entrance door. I tried it. It was locked. I said to Joanna that a little bit of breaking and entering was going to be called for. She said she couldn't think straight, she was so nervous. I asked her to try not to worry. I told her I was going to break the window on the door but that I would try to do it as quietly as possible. We moved away from the front of the block as I searched the ground for something that would do the job in hand. There were lots of small pieces of rubble and concrete around. At last, I found what looked like a suitable projectile. I suggested to Joanna that it might be an idea if she crouched behind a nearby wall. I went to within two yards of the front door of the building. I thought for a second about what I would have to do. When my thoughts were fairly clear, I told myself to just go for it. I simply threw the piece of concrete as hard as I could towards the door. There was a loud bang as the glass shattered. I ran and joined Joanna behind the wall.

'Not quite what I'd expected,' I said.

'That must have been heard by just about everybody in the area,' Joanna said.

'Not to worry,' I said, 'we'll sit tight for a while.'

After about fifteen minutes of nobody appearing, I got up and had a look around. All was quiet. 'Let's go,' I said. The upper part of the entrance door had gone almost completely. I carefully stretched my hand inside. I beckoned Joanna, opened the door and went inside. There were just two doors on the bottom floor. I tested the one on the left. It was unlocked. 'We're in luck,' I said to Joanna. We stepped inside. It was very dark. I managed to find a light switch and clicked it on. We were inside a large living room. There was a table, a large armchair and a couple of side chairs.

'Well, it's not quite the Hilton, but I think it will do for the night. What do you think?'

'It'll have to do,' said Joanna, 'it's better than nothing.'

'How are you?' I asked. 'Are you okay?'

'Yes, I'm fine,' replied Joanna, 'just a bit confused and nervy, that's all.'

There was a huge glass ashtray and a lamp on the table. I put the lamp on and extinguished the central light. Surprisingly, there were curtains at the window. Joanna closed them. I said to Joanna that she could have the armchair and that I would take a side chair. She quickly replied that there was room enough for two on the armchair. I didn't argue.

'What do you think about that little bit of nonsense with Abdul?' I asked.

'Oh, he's just an opportunistic petty thief. He probably took up cab driving with mugging in mind. After all, people leaving the country are ideal targets. They almost certainly have a fair bit of cash on them, and they just want to get away. They wouldn't want to about-turn and go back just to get involved in petty crime proceedings. Will he be okay there?'

'Yes,' I said. 'When he doesn't radio in to say that he's arrived at the airport, they'll immediately be out looking for him. By the way, what did you say to Abdul that him to comply so willingly? It crossed my mind that he might doubt whether you had the bottle to use the gun.'

'I told him I was a trained markswoman,' replied Joanna, 'And that I would have no hesitation in blowing him away if I felt I had to.'

'What do we do in the morning?' asked Joanna.

'I don't know. I'll think of something.'

I think I was just about ready to drop off when I heard voices outside. The door of the flat swung open and two men came inside. The bigger of the two immediately pulled a pistol and pointed it towards us. They were wearing slightly baggy trousers, heavy jackets and small round caps. Both had beards. The man with the gun asked us what we were doing in this building. I replied that we simply needed somewhere for the night. The two men spoke loudly to each other in Arabic. The big man handed the gun to his smaller companion. At this he left. The smaller man picked up one of the side chairs and sat at the table opposite us. He kept the pistol pointing straight at us.

After several minutes of silence, Joanna said something in Arabic to our guard. He replied.

Soon, there was a conversation going on between them. I wondered what Joanna was playing at. Somehow I felt I would not have approved of what they were saying to each other. It all sounded a bit too cosy for my liking. Suddenly, they stood up. Joanna glanced briefly towards me. She coughed. I could have sworn she said 'ashtray' through her cough. I wondered about this. It didn't make sense. Joanna and her new friend walked towards the hall that gave access to the flat's other rooms. I guessed that they went into a bedroom. I sat gazing blankly across the living room, stunned by what I had just witnessed. Oh, my God, I said to myself, when I suddenly realised what Joanna was probably doing. I hope I'm not too late. I picked up the ashtray and crept towards the bedroom. In the hall, the first door on the left was slightly ajar. I peeped in. Joanna and our guard were at the far side of the bedroom, standing by a single bed with a bare mattress on it. Joanna had cleverly arranged her strategic snog with the unsuspecting fly she had lured into her web of sexual promise such that he had his back to the bedroom door. I eased the door slowly open. Don't squeak, please don't squeak. I tiptoed across the room. My pulse was thumping all over my body. I felt I had no strength. By now Joanna was moaning quite loudly. Brilliant. I was glad my intended victim was wearing a cap and hoped this would protect his head to some extent. Trembling like a newborn kitten, I raised the ashtray and dropped it heavily onto Joanna's temporary boyfriend's head. He immediately crumpled and fell to the floor. I just stood there, rooted. I must have looked like the statue of a man who had just thumped a man with an ashtray. Joanna took the ashtray out of my hand and laid it on the bed. 'Come on, let's get out of here,' she said.

We got out of that place at the double. We half-walked and half-ran through deserted, shadowy back streets. We were both well aware that the knowledge we had just gained about the location of the terrorist's HQ meant that our lives were in jeopardy. I wasn't bothered about the direction we were taking. I just wanted away. Eventually and inevitably we ran out of steam. I looked around but could see no place where we could take the weight off our feet. With a bottom at either end we managed to sit back to back on Joanna's case. I removed my *dishdasha.* I realised that wearing a *dishdasha* without a *ghatra* would attract attention.

I asked Joanna how she was. She said she was fine. 'Well, that sure was a scary little episode,' I said.

'I think we were very unlucky to have stumbled into that place,' said Joanna.

'Yes, that's what I thought. That means there are now two organisations after my blood.'

'I'm bound to be a target too, now,' said Joanna.

'Maybe we should split up,' I suggested. 'The terrorists saw you wearing a headscarf, without it they probably wouldn't recognise you. And they don't know where you work or live. As for Nigel, if he were to ask probing questions, your saying that you had simply gone to the airport to see me off would be entirely credible.'

'I'm coming with you,' replied Joanna firmly.

'Well, if you're absolutely sure. By the way, how did you get that bloke to fall into your little trap?'

'I told him I fancied him.'

'How did you get him to leave me there unguarded?'

'I convinced him that you wouldn't leave without me, and that you wouldn't try to alert the police in case it put me in danger.'

'Brilliant,' I said. 'By the way, why did the big bloke leave the flat so quickly?'

'He told the little guy he would have to go to consult with the leader.'

'Oh, of course.'

'Anyway, what next?' asked Joanna.

'Well, it seems to me that the only way out of Kuwait now is by boat.'

'A what?' exclaimed Joanna, 'Where the hell are we going to get our hands on a boat?'

'Somewhere south of Salyma, where the Gulf Road bends, there is a small marina. We could nick one from there. So, all we've got to do now is get to the

Gulf Road from here. If we keep going east we must hit it.' We seemed to be on a link road between two major roads. We looked around and agreed which direction east was.

While I was looking in what we had established was an easterly direction, I saw a car pass on that main road. It was travelling very slowly. A few minutes later, another car passed going in the opposite direction. It was also travelling very slowly. I was certain it was the same car. It had to be either the CIA or the terrorists. I didn't say a word about this to Joanna. I asked Joanna if she felt up to making a move. She removed her headscarf and hitched her skirt up to knee length. We plodded on and somehow got ourselves onto the main road that I had seen to the West. I didn't like this, but Joanna said it was familiar to her and that she was certain it led to Salyma. There was light traffic, and every car that passed jangled my already knotted nerves. The road was dead straight. Ahead, in the distance, I could see a traffic-lighted junction. We made painfully slow progress towards this. It was further away than it had first looked. When we got to within a dozen or so yards of the junction, I jogged on. Something told me I was going to see something that would be to my liking. When I got to the lights I looked left. At the end of that road there were big, bright street lights. I said several yeses to myself. It was the Gulf Road. Again, this side road seemed like a giant treadmill. The Gulf Road lights didn't seem to be getting any nearer. I asked Joanna a couple of times if she felt she needed a little rest. Each time she said no. This was disappointing because I felt I needed one myself. Eventually, we got to the Gulf Motorway. It was empty. We turned right into Gulf Road, there was a low wall running along the inside edge of the pavement. I suggested a stop. I eased myself down onto the wall. It could well have been a luxury sofa. Joanna sat next to me. I opened my bag and dug out a couple of cans of cola. I drew Joanna's attention to the glowing announcement over the Gulf that day was about to break.

'Last lap, darling,' I said.

'An uplifting thought until one reminds oneself that the A to B you refer to as the last lap is going to seem like a circumnavigation of the globe. By the way, do you know how to start the engine and steer a boat?'

'Oh, my plan doesn't involve a motor boat. What I have in mind is something rather smaller than that.'

'Smaller?'

'Yes, a rowing boat.'

'What?' exclaimed Joanna, 'You're mad.'

'Think about it this way, Joanna,' I said. 'If the boat were to run out of petrol we would just drift, and God only knows where we'd end up. In a rowing boat we can't run out of power.'

'Power? After two days in the middle of the Gulf in a rowing boat we'll be frazzled, dehydrated and dead. More importantly, your perception of me would drop below recoverable depths if you were to catch a glimpse of me sitting with my stern over the stern several times a day. Why risk rowing down the Gulf, anyway? My flat can't be that far from here. Why don't we hide up there for a few days at least?'

'Think about it, Joanna. I didn't appear at the airport. So, they know I'm still in Kuwait. And, when you don't turn up at the College tomorrow and don't phone in to say you're sick, they'll put two and two together. Your flat is the obvious hiding place. Before tomorrow is out they'll be knocking on your door.'

Before I could try to reassure Joanna that escaping down the Gulf would be safe enough, I caught the dark image of an approaching car out of the corner of my eye. I glanced towards it. It seemed to be slowing. I numbed. We couldn't run. We couldn't hide. I told Joanna to look down. The car drew up right in front of us. 'Hello, Mr. Jack,' said somebody inside the car. I could hardly believe my ears. I was sure I recognised the voice. I looked up. It was Ali, one of my students, and his wife.

'Where are you off to at such an early hour?' I asked. 'The cockerels are still in bed.'

'I go to Bahrain, Mr. Jack. Where do you go to?'

'Amazingly, I'm also going to Bahrain,' I replied.
'I take you to Bahrain, Mr. Jack'.
'But I don't have a visa or papers or anything, Ali.'
'No problem, Mr. Jack, you are safe in car.'
'But the border guards would be bound to see me and ask me for my papers.'
'No, no, Mr. Jack, they do not see you. You are in back of car.'
I suddenly realised Ali was offering me a lift in his boot. I pondered the idea for a few seconds. It would be extremely risky, but it might just work. I felt I had little choice. I had to get out of Kuwait. I turned to Joanna and checked that she understood what Ali was proposing. She nodded. I put it to Ali that even in the boot the border guards would be bound to find me when they searched the car. Ali insisted that this would not happen. He said he travelled to Bahrain every month, he and the guards knew each other well and that they were his friends. He said they sometimes checked the car on the way back but never on the way down to Bahrain. I decided to go for it and told Joanna.
'So, now we do have to part,' I said. 'There's no way you could go through with this.'
'Oh, I can rough it if I have to,' protested Joanna.
'It's not the discomfort,' I explained, 'it's the risk. It is far too risky. If we were to get caught, the Saudi authorities would charge us with every crime in the book. I could get slung in prison and virtually

forgotten about. The thought of you in prison terrifies me. Please go back, Joanna. You'll be safe. You could probably turn up at the College this morning as if nothing had happened.'

'Okay then, you're probably right.'

I told Ali that I would travel with him, but asked him if he would first take Joanna back to her flat in Salyma. He right away agreed to this. We dumped our cases in the boot, got into Ali's car and set off.

After about a mile, at a set of lights, we turned right. After another mile or so Joanna said she was now in familiar territory and started to give Ali directions. I asked Joanna if she would write to me. She said of course she would. I gave her my parents' address and said I would give them my new address as soon as I was settled in London. I told Joanna I would write to her anonymously and that this was because I felt it was likely that the College's incoming mail was being intercepted and read. I had no doubt that my own letters were being opened prior to their arrival at my mailbox. In no time, we were pulling up outside Joanna's flat. Ali immediately got out and went round to the back of the car. Joanna and I followed. As Joanna lifted her case out of the boot, Ali offered to take it upstairs for her. She declined, saying that she would manage okay. Ali got back into the front of the car. I turned to Joanna. 'This is it then,' I said. 'This is goodbye.'

'Au revoir, silly,' she replied, 'au revoir.'

‘Of course,’ I said. All of a sudden there was a lump in my throat and I was aching inside.

I looked into Joanna’s eyes. We hugged and kissed. Ali returned with a large bottle of water and placed it into the boot. He turned to me and gave me a ‘let’s go’ look.

‘Bye then, darling, take care.’

‘You too,’ said Joanna. Joanna clasped me briefly and placed a butterfly kiss on the corner of my mouth. I clambered into the boot and tried to make myself comfortable. I again looked into Joanna’s eyes. She smiled and gave me a little wave. She didn’t seem at all upset by my leaving. While I was still gazing towards Joanna, Ali put his hand up onto the boot lid and slammed me into blackness.

Chapter Nine

What the hell am I doing here? Life… What's it all about? I come out to Kuwait, a very ordinary bloke, a little bit of an adventure, a much-needed job, earn a bit of dosh, meet some new people, and what happens? I walked straight into the scheming clutches of totally ruthless people, conned, set up, the proverbial lamb to the slaughter. But I was lucky. I sussed them before they could close in on me. Not so George. I wonder where he is right now? Probably crouched in the corner of a room somewhere. A twittering heap. Totally brainwashed. Constantly mumbling 'death to Saddam.' Well, maybe not that bad. But bad enough. If the CIA put their deadly plan into action it is most unlikely that George will get out of Iraq alive. What could George have ever done to deserve such a fate? A great bloke. I wish I could have seen the light sooner so that I could have warned him. But then, would he have listened? He would probably have laughed in my face. I was lucky. The real reason for our recruitment became terrifyingly clear to me just in time. I was able to escape, touch wood. But at what price? I'd just about given up all hope of ever meeting my perfect partner, I come out to Kuwait expecting a monastic existence, my mind set accordingly, and, here she is. She's out of my class but so what, she takes to me. Then just as we're getting close we're torn apart. How sadistic can you get? Now I know how Tantalus felt.

About an hour after setting off, the car stopped. I could hear voices. My body numbed. This had to be the Saudi border. Before long, we moved off. We'd got through okay.

I had no sooner started feeling good about getting through the border when I suddenly realised that this now made me an illegal immigrant in a closed country. How long would this last? I hadn't thought to ask Ali how long it would take to get to Bahrain. Would I survive in this metal box? It was already starting to get stuffy. If I started to suffocate would Ali hear me knocking? I'll just have to try to cross that bridge if and when I come to it.

At last the car stopped. A second later, Ali opened the boot and invited me to come out. He apologised for having kept me in for so long, and explained that he had to get well clear of a large military base just inside the Saudi border. I got into the back seat. At this point, the Gulf Road was running between the Gulf on the left and on the right a high wire fence surrounding a huge oil field. Thankfully, the sun was being denied giving a demonstration of its full thermal might by thin veils of cloud.

As we got further south, the number and the size of the settlements near the Gulf Road increased. Small villages, then small towns. After cruising swiftly along for about a couple of hours, without warning Ali turned the car off the motorway and into a quiet-looking side street. Saying nothing, Ali got out of the car and disappeared into a small shop. A few minutes later he re-emerged carrying a poly bag. This turned out to be full of pitta-bread sandwiches and cans of lemonade. Sitting there, we had a most enjoyable snack lunch. When the lemonade had been guzzled, Ali's wife dug out a flask and some paper cups from her bag and treated us to some coffee. This was strong, black and very sweet. Ali mentioned that there was a toilet in the shop and we each grabbed the opportunity to pay this a visit. Before long, we were back on the highway in. We had another stop an hour further down the road. Again we had some drinks and I stretched my legs outside the car. Back in the car, clearly exhausted by recent events, I immediately fell asleep. Within just a few minutes of my coming round, Ali looked round and made the dreaded announcement that I would now have to get back into the trunk. And, as I immediately discovered, outside the car it was now extremely hot. But, back into the stifling blackness of the boot it had to be.

s we continued, literally by the minute, my environment became increasingly unpleasant. Also, I still felt very tired and was tempted to allow myself to drop off to sleep again, but something told me not to. I could hear that there was now a bit of traffic on the road, and I found myself listening to the crude music that many different cars and lorries were creating. Eventually, in near desperation I started searching the floor of the boot for any small splits or holes through which even the tiniest amount of fresh air might be coming. Amazingly, I found a seam of welding that was badly pitted. The idea of drilling through these flawed bits came to me and, with the drill bit in my Swiss Army knife, I managed to open up a couple of quite good supplies of air. I immediately crouched down and got my nose directly over the two holes I had just made.

The car started stopping and starting every few seconds. We had to be near the centre of a fairly large town, possibly Al Khobar. I hoped it was. This was the nearest town to the start of the causeway over to Bahrain. The car stopped again. This time there were voices. It had to be another border post. Yet again, my body stiffened with fear. I felt like a tiny mouse sleekitly cowering in a hidey-hole, waiting and listening for the all-clear. Though terrified, at the same time I felt like giving myself up just to get some fresh air. The car set off again. Again I felt the relaxation of relief flood through my body. I wondered about my petrified response to the dangerous situation I had just been in. I remember being told that when we stepped into a dangerous situation we immediately stiffened to make ourselves less conspicuous. Apparently some animals have difficulty in seeing things that are not moving. The bumping up of the pulse rate is our body preparing us to fight or run away. But why did my pulse start thumping all over my body just then? I wasn't about to fight anybody or go anywhere. And, my body well knew this. So why did it prepare me for something it well knew wasn't about to happen? It should have put me into an almost comatose state so that I wouldn't make a noisy move. Maybe the brain came to the conclusion millions of years ago that in any dangerous situation, no matter how hopeless, it would be as well to get the body into a high state of readiness. Just in case.

I was just about to pass out when the car stopped again. My senses immediately went back to red alert. I heard the handle of the boot being turned. I didn't panic. The boot opened. But the line of light that was created didn't get more than an inch wide. Ali's voice said, 'Okay, Mr. Jack.' In no time, we were back on the move. I didn't dare raise my head in case I hit the lid of the boot and sprang it wide open. But, with half an eye over the tailgate I could see we were on a motorway. This had to be the causeway. The only buildings I could see were far in the distance, and I could see nothing either side of the motorway. After maybe an hour on the causeway, Ali stopped the car and came round and closed the boot. He told me we did not have far to go now. Another fifteen minutes later we stopped again. There were voices. This had to be the border post into Bahrain. Again I froze as I waited for the boot to be opened. It didn't happen. After this we seemed to enter light traffic, turning left, turning right and occasionally stopping.

Eventually, the car stopped and remained still for several minutes. All was quiet. Surely this is journey's end, I said to myself. The boot opened, and a beaming Ali told me that we were now in Bahrain. The pain of the brightness of the afternoon sun forced me to close my eyes for a while. I stretched the stiffness out of my joints and climbed out of the boot. I thanked Ali and shook his hand. He simply said I was very welcome. I looked around. Ali had stopped the car on a strip of land between the sea and a coast road. Underfoot the soil was firm and ashy. The car was parked right by the water's edge. The coast road bordered what seemed to be Bahrain's commercial district. There were many tall buildings. From where I was standing, I could see several office blocks, hotels, restaurants, a bank and an airline office.

Ahead, at a junction on the coast road, a side street led to what looked like a busy city centre street. Ali pointed out a hotel. 'That is good hotel,' he said. 'You stay there, the Oasis.' I shook Ali's hand warmly, thanked him again, and said goodbye to him and his wife. In no time, Ali was in his car and away. I immediately set off towards the hotel that Ali had recommended.

I walked past on the left a delightful green and leafy town centre square. At the top of the street I was directly across from the Oasis Hotel. I crossed the busy road. I found the entrance to the hotel in the street running down the side. The hotel reception was immediately inside.

Putting on a smile, I asked the receptionist if he had a single room. He immediately asked for my passport. Oh-oh, I said to myself, here we go again. Realising I had little choice in the matter I dug out my passport and handed it over. Oh my God, I thought, if he checks my movements he is going to ask how I got into Bahrain. What do I say? Not much I can say. Maybe he is bribable. I watched him closely, my face taut with fear. He opened the passport, read page one and closed it. The receptionist looked up at me and smiled. 'You have room booked, Sir,' he said. 'Number six-o-five. You go on up, please, Sir. I keep passport here.'

For several seconds I stood at the front of the reception desk, rooted, trying to make sense of what I had just heard. But it soon became obvious that I hadn't escaped from Kuwait at all. Far from it. They had probably followed me the whole way. Now they were delighting in terrorising me by letting me know that they were waiting for me. There was no point in trying to make a run for it, I immediately decided. There were sure to be a couple of heavies outside the hotel right now. Feeling emotionally drained, and still fuzzyheaded, I turned and drifted towards the lift. As I did so, my eye caught sight of a notice on the wall which stated that there was a bar and restaurant on the second floor. Instantly, I could see a pint of golden lager. No point in rushing into the slaughter, I said to myself. I'll have a last-request pint.

In the bar, there were only six Arab blokes sitting in a circle, each with at least one whiskey in front of him. All were smoking. I sat on a stool at the bar and answered the smiling barmaid's, 'Yes Sir?' with a request for a pint of lager. While she was pouring, I discovered that her name was Fiona and that she was from Edinburgh. I simplified my circumstances by stating that I was travelling and just passing through. I downed my pint in what must have been personal record time. As soon as I had placed my empty glass back onto the bar, Fiona lifted it and said, 'Same again?'

'Sure, I badly need it.'

'You haven't just come across the desert on foot, have you?'

'No,' I replied wondering why she had asked that specific question. I decided to savour my second pint. I was, after all, in no hurry.

How could they have known for sure that I would come into this hotel? Of course, they didn't. I didn't know I was coming here myself. It was Ali. Ali led me here. Even Ali must be on their payroll. My God, who else is on it? I wondered what they would do with me. A simple bump-off job, probably. Maybe an injection of a lethal drug. Then, into the big suitcase. A suitcase that would then be dropped into the Gulf after dark. Maybe not. Maybe they'll still regard me as potentially useful to them. After all, I could still be brainwashed. I could still be made to do their dirty work for them.

Why did the Yanks want the Brits to do their dirty work for them? Of course, I suddenly realised, sending in military men, Americans or Arabs, could have adverse long-term political repercussions. If the Brits get captured, deny all knowledge of them. Argue that they must have been acting on their own.

I wondered whether in the event of my surviving the mission I would get my old self back. Probably not. I'd probably end up in a home for the hopelessly bewildered in Cairo or Tunis. Presumably, at some point my parents will make enquiries to the College as to my whereabouts. The College will probably just tell them that I left Kuwait without notice and that they had no idea where I had gone. Anyway, the mission has probably been designed as a suicide one. The hit will probably involve my having grenades round my waist, something like that. But it didn't matter. Soon, effectively, my life will be over.

I wondered why I wasn't desperately thinking of a way to escape. A slip out of a toilet window, some sort of new disguise or a quick dash for it. Where was fight or flight now? It would all be totally futile. That's what it was. No matter where I went, they would seek me out and inevitably find me. There's no escaping the CIA. You are living up a tiny tributary of the Amazon with a small tribe who live on monkey meat and insects when one morning a small boy runs into your hut and tells you that a pale-faced man has arrived in the next village asking everybody if they have seen a white man. You've been expecting and waiting for this moment every morning for the past 23 years. There's no more running. You're tired of running. You have to face him. You confront him. He said he's come to take you in. You ask him if he couldn't just leave you in peace with your wife and six children, pass on by and report back that he had found nothing. He said he would love to, and would if he could but, alas, he had his job to do. You admire his integrity and commitment. You thank him and say you'll come quietly. You ask for one more hour with your family. With a facial expression that in a movie would melt the hearts of a cinema full of Hannibal Lechters, he nods.

In a daze of total demoralisation, I slid off my stool and left the bar. When I got to the lift I about-turned, went back to the bar, picked up my case and returned to the lift. I took the lift to the sixth floor, looked for and quickly found room five. I stood blindly gazing at the door for several minutes. I knocked. A female voice called from inside 'come on in.' I couldn't believe my ears. It sounded like Joanna. I told myself it couldn't possibly be. The door opened. It was Joanna.

'What kept you?' she asked, with a broad smile and chuckle. I couldn't speak. God only knows what I must have looked like at that point. A gawking frog. Joanna grasped my arm and led me into the room.

'What are you doing here?' I asked. 'How did you get here?'

'I flew. No problem.' As Joanna spoke, she dug clothes out of my bag and put them into drawers and into a wardrobe. 'I've been here for a couple of hours. I even had time to pop into the College to check my mailbox before my flight. There was a letter from Sally, by the way. She sends her love. She's getting married in the autumn. Not coming back to Kuwait.'

'But how did you know I would be here?'

'I didn't. I told Ali to send you here.'

'When?'

'As soon as you were out of the way and into Ali's boot. I know this place well. I stayed here several times. It has an excellent restaurant. We're spoiled for choice, in fact. There's an excellent Indian restaurant just across the road.'

I still wasn't thinking clearly. But I was delighted to discover from Joanna's story that Ali wasn't some kind of CIA lackey. Also, it meant that the CIA weren't immediately on my tail. Joanna asked me how I felt now that I had successfully escaped.

'Well, albeit entirely by luck, I got out of Kuwait and into Bahrain. So good so far. But my problems are by no means over. How do I get out? I didn't give this any thought at all when I was in Kuwait, and shortly after my arrival in Bahrain it looked like I was going to be leaving Bahrain in a suitcase.'

'Yes, I saw that fly in the ointment of your plan for getting back to the UK, and I attended to it.' Joanna went into her shoulder bag and came out with a passport. 'There you are,' she said, handing the passport to me.

Baffled, and in several minds as to what I might find inside, I opened the passport. It was a perfect duplicate of my own. It even had a Bahraini immigration stamp with the correct date. 'Where the hell did you get that from?'

'Don't ask.'

'Oh, I see.'

'Lets just say that if you have the money, there's practically nothing you cannot get.'

'But this is a work of art, how long did it take to get made up?'

'While I waited'.

'Amazing', I said.

'Just make sure you don't get the two documents mixed up. Stuff the genuine one into a toilet bag or something.'

'How did you get hold of a photograph?'

'That wasn't too difficult, actually. Two of the heap of photos you brought out to Kuwait with you came to the College. These went on to your file, and every teacher's file is kept in the filing cabinet in Nigel's office. So, when Nigel was out of his office I popped in. Simple. Like the way you got your passport back.'

'How do you know how I got my passport back?'

'Well, it's very obvious. There's no other way you could have got it back.'

I had difficulty in taking in what had just happened, but for the first time in a long time I felt optimistic and good inside.

My eyes were having trouble convincing my brain that the here and now information they were passing into it was real. Here I was in a hotel room with Joanna. And, I knew I was soon going to have to try to accept the fact it was our room. The confirmation that it was our room came when Joanna went into the wardrobe and pulled out her case.

'Now, I'm going to need a top and you're going to need a shirt for tonight,' she said. 'So, where's that little travelling iron of mine?' Joanna got a tiny yellow iron out of her case and started looking around for a socket. My eyes slavishly followed her just as they had been doing since I entered the room.

One entire wall of the room was a window. Part of this was a sliding glass door. I pulled this back just enough to step out onto what was a fairly large veranda. I was immediately above a major city street. But, as if by design, there were no buildings immediately opposite. The square that I had come past earlier gave the hotel a magnificent view towards the Gulf. I felt like pinching myself. Just an hour or so ago I was still on the run from the CIA. Now I was in circumstances that were beautiful and unthreatening. Just a few months ago I laid eyes on Joanna for the first time. It was a stunning experience. Since then we've become good friends. But, as far as I was concerned, getting any closer to Joanna would have required my successfully reaching and entering another world. Now, here I was sharing a room with her. I must be doing something right. I turned and went back into the room.

'There you go,' said Joanna, hanging my shirt on the handle of the wardrobe. I thanked her.

'Right,' I said, 'I'm badly needing a shower.'

'Me too,' said Joanna. 'And, since only about half the spray hits the body while the other half goes straight down the plughole when just one person is having a shower, in the interest of Bahraini water conservation in particular, I suggest we have our shower together. Unless of course you're not much interested in conservation. Are you?'

'Hugely.'

Chapter Ten

That evening, we opted for the Indian. It was a rather unusual place. The walls were bright red and, throughout, the woodwork was black. There was a space in the middle of the room, which could only have been a small dance floor, but nobody danced. On a low platform a trio of musicians played delightfully haunting traditional Indian music. The wine and the food were excellent. Everything about Joanna was a joy. She seemed happy and contented. This made me feel good. I felt relaxed and excited at the same time. I kept wondering what I had done to deserve such happy times. We chatted and laughed almost non-stop. I wondered at what point I would be able to start thinking of Joanna as my girlfriend or my partner. She had followed me to Bahrain. Surely that meant something. Nothing had been said thus far. But even now I seemed to know that I would only ever be able to think of Joanna as mine in the way that the wonders and beauties of nature were mine, and that I would be thankful for and treasure every day we were together. When she went away I would be left hoping and praying that she would return. And I would thank God when she did so. I knew it wasn't me, but I told myself to try to take each day as it came.

'What do you think about Sally getting married?' asked Joanna.

'Great,' I replied.

'Not disappointed?'

'Not at all, why should I be?'

'You and she were quite close friends.'

'Yes, but that's all we were. Just pals. I hope she has a very happy future.'

'And what about us?' Joanna asked. I could hardly believe my ears. Was she really asking about whether we ought to settle down together?

'What do you mean?' I asked.

'Our immediate plans,' she replied. 'How long are we going to stay in Bahrain?'

'I thought we could spend two or three days here.'

'Good-o,' said Joanna, 'I like it here.'

When we left the restaurant we giggled and laughed as we crossed to the hotel. In the lift, the confined space seemed to throw us together, and we hugged and kissed our way to the sixth floor. We agreed it was too early to go to bed.

'What'll we do?' I asked.

'Drink?' suggested Joanna.

'Good idea,' I replied. 'Let's phone room service.'

In next to no time, a half bottle of whiskey and two glasses arrived. I gave the young man a one-dinar note. As I went back into the room I kicked myself for getting it wrong again. One dinar equals two pounds, I reminded myself, not the other way round.

Joanna and I managed to squeeze ourselves onto the one easy chair that was in the room. As the late evening gave way to the wee small hours, the topics of conversation between Joanna and I became more serious. Joanna asked what we would do when we got back to the UK. I suggested we rent a flat, possibly in Chiswick, which I knew well. Joanna quickly agreed. We agreed that our next priority would be to get jobs. Joanna suggested that, if we could build up sufficient funds, we could buy our own place. I agreed. Suddenly, quite out of the blue, Joanna said she loved me.

'How about you?' she asked.

'Yes, I love me too,' I replied. Even as I spoke I knew I was having a rush of stupidity to the head. But the words were out before I could stop them. I immediately apologized, but it was too late, the damage had been done. Joanna's silence told me that my words had been hurtful. A perfect opportunity to let Joanna know my true feelings for her, and I blow it. Typical.

I think we managed to finish the half bottle between us. In the morning, the bottle and the glasses had gone. So had Joanna. Her side of the bed was still warm.

Suddenly, the door opened and in walked Joanna carrying a tray full of breakfast. She had managed to cram everything onto the tray. Coffee, toast, marmalade, the lot.

'Out,' said Joanna.

'What, not breakfast in bed?' I asked.

'Nope,' she said.

We had breakfast at a small table by the window. It was another perfect moment. The street below was already busy. For some reason, I kept peering through the net curtain at the large hotel across the road, just to the left. It was at right-angles to our hotel, on the street I had come up the day before, overlooking the square. A man leaving the hotel caught my eye. He looked vaguely familiar. Eventually, I could see who it was. I hoped I was wrong. I got up. The sliding window was about a foot open. I peeped round the edge. Oh my God, I said to myself, it is. It's David. I went back to my chair.

'You look as though you've just seen a ghost,' said Joanna.

'I wish I had,' I replied.

'What have you seen?' asked Joanna.

'Not what, who.'

'Okay then, who?'

'Only David, that's who.'

'But why should David's being here be a cause for concern? Surely he isn't any sort of threat to us.'

'He is, believe me, he is. He's after me. He's followed me here.'

'But David, like many of the teachers, comes down here almost every other weekend.'

'But why is he staying at the Belmont?'

'He probably stays there every time.'

'It's too much of a coincidence and I can't take any chances. I've got to get out of here, and quick.'

Joanna protested briefly, then suddenly stopped. 'Okay,' she said firmly, 'I'll go straight along to the airline office and get tickets for the first flight out of Bahrain.'

I suspected Joanna was now humouring me. But I didn't care. I just knew I couldn't take any chances. Joanna stood up and went to the bathroom. Within an hour she was dressed and ready to go. 'Won't be long,' she said.

'Take care,' I said. I sat on the edge of the bed thinking about this latest twist in the story of my escape from the Middle East. I just wanted to be back on English soil. For some reason I felt compelled to take another look into the street. I needed a double take on what I saw. It was David and Joanna, chatting, bold as brass right in front of the hotel. I drew back into the room. Then I thought to myself, what's the point? He knows all about my being here. I might as well go out onto the veranda and give him a wave and a great-to-see-you smile. I sat tight. I looked at the phone in the room. That's why Joanna didn't phone the airline office, she wanted to meet David. Those two could well have flown down to Bahrain together. Into my mind loomed the fact it was Joanna who got me into this place. The receptionist is probably a CIA agent. As soon as I arrived, he probably phoned Kuwait. I wondered if I was going crazy. Everything that was happening around me now seemed to be suspicious and threatening. I told myself to pull myself together.

I didn't have to wait long for Joanna's return. As soon as she entered the room I asked her how she had got on.

'No problem,' she replied. 'Got the tickets. One o'clock flight this afternoon.' I deliberately didn't say another word. I waited. 'By the way,' Joanna said, 'I bumped into David. I tried to avoid him, but couldn't, he spotted me from across the street.'

'Did he ask you why you were in Bahrain?'

'Of course he did. I told him I was just having yet another weekend break in the place.'

'Didn't he ask you about your leaving the College?'

'No, of course he didn't. Nobody knows yet.'

As ever, I found I couldn't distrust Joanna. I seemed to know that every word she said was true. Maybe I was wrong about David. Maybe his being here is a coincidence after all. The flight is booked. We'll be leaving soon, and back in the UK before the day is out.

We packed straight away and went down to check out. The bill for the room was much as I had expected, but the price of the night before's whiskey almost brought a tear to my eye. However, there was no way I was going to look like a cheapskate with Joanna there. So, I paid up with as broad a smile as I could manage. In any case, my priority was the return of my passport, and it felt good to have it back on board. Immediately outside the hotel Joanna took my passport and put it into an inside pocket in her jacket. Joanna had agreed to my suggestion of not getting to the airport until the last minute. We went for a wander round the old souk. I bought Joanna a silk scarf. She seemed to really like it. But then, she chose it herself. We managed to kill about an hour in a junk-food place. Avoiding the serious rubbish, we had a coffee and some chips, followed by another coffee.

I was very nervy in the taxi on the way to the airport. Seemingly detecting this, Joanna snuggled close to me and laid her head on my shoulder a couple of times. The near emptiness of the airport set my nerves off again. However, having arrived late we were able to check in immediately. While Joanna was checking in I felt cool and confident. However, I soon discovered how frightening it was to hand over a false passport. The airline person seemed to spend ages checking my personal details. My mouthed dried. My pulse thumped. She turned a few pages and hesitated. I looked on anxiously. She turned a few more pages and hesitated again. At long last she smiled and handed me my passport and boarding pass. Thank God, I said to myself. We went straight to Departures. We bought some duty-free booze and had only just finished a coffee when the boarding calls for our flight began. The nearer I got to the plane the better I felt. By the time we had settled into our seats I was feeling fairly relaxed. But it was only when the plane was pulling itself up and away from the airport that I began to feel the release of the nervous tension and anxiety that had been bottled up inside me. I turned to Joanna. She smiled. 'How are you feeling?' I asked.

'Great,' Joanna replied, 'How about you?'

'I feel wonderful.'

Chapter Eleven

At Schiphol, Joanna and I had recovered our luggage from the carousel in the arrivals hall and had set off in search of BA's check-in when a sudden thought brought me to a stop. This is exactly what they're expecting me to do, I said to myself. Realising she was walking by herself, Joanna stopped and turned. 'What is it?' she asked. I walked slowly towards her.

'I can't go on,' I said.

'What do you mean?' Joanna asked.

'To London. They'll be waiting for me there.' The mental state immediately expressed on Joanna's face was, unmistakably, exasperation. She sighed heavily. She's beginning to tire of me, I said to myself. I wish she could see and accept that I'm only doing what I have to do.

'What makes you think they'll be waiting for you at Heathrow?'

'Well, they don't know exactly how I got out of Kuwait. So they would only be able to guess where I headed for. But they know they don't have to search all over Europe for me. Without a job, and money running out, they know that sooner or later I'll have to head for home. And, they'll probably calculate that this will be sooner.'

'But why would they still be interested in you? You're of no use to them now. You're out of their grasp. And, you don't have any special expertise that they need. If they want somebody else they'll simply wait for a new teacher to start at the College.'

'Yes, I do not have any expertise, Joanna, but they now want to get their hands on me more than ever. I have knowledge. I know what they're up to. And they'll want to gag me, for good. In Kuwait it was my freedom and my sanity that I was in danger of losing. Now it's my life.' Joanna smiled. I was shocked by this, but for some reason or another I simply ignored it. 'You'd better go on alone,' I said. 'You'll be safe. They're not interested in you.'

'On the contrary, my dear Jack,' Joanna said. 'Think about it. Your pursuers will put two and two together and come up with the answer that you and I at least left Kuwait together. So, they now know they only have to find me to find you. They may accept that I know nothing about your reasons for wanting to leave Kuwait, but they will never accept that I don't know where you are. They'll simply beat your whereabouts out of me.'

'Oh, my God, I hadn't thought of that,' I found myself saying. I threw my arms round Joanna, hugged her and apologised for getting her into such a mess.

'Don't be silly,' she said. 'You didn't drag me with you. I'm with you because I

want to be. So, where to now?'
'I suggest we lie low in Amsterdam for a few weeks.'
'Lying low in Amsterdam sounds good to me,' said Joanna.
'Right, Amsterdam here we come.'

We took the train into Amsterdam. Outside *Centraal* station we stopped, laid down our luggage and looked around. The station was close to where a major canal flowed into Amsterdam harbour. On the far side of the canal there was an extensive terrace of assorted buildings. We scanned these. Our agreed priority was to quickly find a place for the night. Joanna said that she had been in Amsterdam several times before and added that she remembered there being a small backpackers' hotel in this area.
She pointed to a very narrow building.
'I think that's it, ' she said.
'Lets check it out,' I said. As we crossed the wide, flat bridge, I found amusing the number of bicycles that were parked against each other and ultimately against the canal railings. I guessed they belonged to people who travelled to work by train. If your bike is against the railings, how do you get it out on days when you get away from work early?
Joanna had guessed well. The unlikely looking building she had pointed to was indeed a small hotel. It was only the width of a one-window shop, but it

was three storeys high with possibly a fourth storey in the roof space. The reception desk was immediately inside the front door. It was all very informal. A young man sitting at the desk told us that it was cash in advance, bed and breakfast. Joanna whispered to me that it would do until we got a chance to look around. I paid the young man, he handed us two keys and told us that our rooms, two singles, were on the third floor.

The stairs were steep and narrow, and on each floor there was a narrow hall giving access to each room. The stairway up to the third floor was a spiral. Right little fire-trap this place, I said to myself. I'd noticed a fire extinguisher on each of the floors, but this did nothing to reassure me. Peeing into a forest fire. Our rooms were exactly opposite each other. We unlocked both and had a look inside. They were practically identical. We opted for the one we had opened up first. In it there was a bed, a bed-side cabinet and a side chair. The bed doubled as seating. We were tired, thirsty and hungry. Joanna volunteered to pop out and do a bit of shopping. No more than ten minutes later she returned with beer and crisps.

By the time we'd had one bottle of beer and a packet of crisps each our eyelids were like lead. With the sun still shining we turned in. And, during the night, probably made the average log look fidgety.

Next morning, we got up early and went down to the hotel's dining room. Over breakfast, which consisted of a boiled egg and a slice of cold ham, Joanna and I discussed our plans for the day. Joanna wanted to do some shopping. I said I fancied a simple sightseeing stroll around the city centre. So, we agreed to go our separate ways.

Joanna suggested that, since the hotel didn't have a bar, one of our first tasks should be to seek out a nearby pub that we could use as a base. I agreed.

The nearest pub to the hotel turned out to be rather glossy-looking place called *The John Barleycorn.* We went in and checked it out. The beer the barman recommended to us was excellent and, despite all the plastic and tubular steel, Joanna and I both felt that the room was reasonably warm and welcoming. So, we decided to make the *John* our local. We arranged to meet there later, between four and five. I walked with Joanna as far as Marks and Spencer's and then set off on my own. I decided to employ a strategy of sticking to the main roads, until I got to know the city better. Anyway, I was enjoying hearing the sound of the bell on the trams as they droned past every few minutes.

This made me feel I was in the past.
And, all the buildings on my route thus far were wonderfully conducive to my feeling that I had wandered into a bygone era. I kept hoping that I

wouldn't encounter a modern carbuncle.

When the major road I was on crossed a canal route, without making any decision to do so, I turned to take a stroll along the banks of the canal. Before stepping out, I stopped briefly to take in the view along the waterway. The narrow canal, its tiny hump-backed bridges, the trees and the terraces of traditional Dutch houses combined to make the scene before me a delightful visual experience. At last, I set off. As I walked, for some unknown reason I found myself constantly drifting towards the edge of the canal and looking down into the water.

So, there I was, strolling along, minding my own business, when suddenly I felt somebody looking at me. I looked round and looked again. I looked away. Was that an hallucination? Or was the image I had just seen real? I looked yet again. Yes,it was real. It was a woman sitting in a window, in her underwear. I was well aware of the fact that Amsterdam had a thriving sex industry, but I found it hard to believe that I was in a red-light district. It seemed too posh to be a red light district. I resumed my stroll. I was approaching a busy point in the canal's route. There was a bridge over which there was a steady stream of people crossing in both directions. There seemed to be several pubs in the area, and many people were sitting at tables close to the edge of the canal. I popped into the first pub I came to, bought myself a beer and was lucky enough to find a free table. As I settled down into my chair I looked around, and, in that brief moment, clocked enough women in windows to leave me in no doubt that the personal services sector was indeed the greatest contributor to the local economy. As I took my first sip of my beer I glanced up and discovered that I was directly opposite a woman in a window on the other side of the canal. I couldn't take my eyes off her. I was mesmerised by her absolute stillness. Potential customers gawked briefly, but not once did she beckon, gesture or even wink an eye. What self control. But what a waste of time. Sitting doing nothing for hours on end in the afternoons. She ought to read. She could do a correspondence course while she's sitting there. Get herself a few qualifications.

Before long, having several scantily clad women on view made me uncomfortable. It was a mind-boggling situation. It was unreal. I decided to venture further along the canal.

The handful of clouds that had been in the sky earlier had melted away. It was a beautiful day. Time for a bit of lunch, I said to myself. At the next bridge over the canal there was an old-fashioned corner café, I went in. It was deserted. Too many tables in the place seemed to emphasise this. I'd always felt there was something sad about an empty café. I hoped things would pick up later. The barman welcomed me.

But he didn't smile. It seemed that false smiling was frowned upon in Amsterdam. I bought some salad sandwiches and a small beer. I went outside and sat at one of the half dozen empty tables by the canal. I had no sooner bottomed-up my glass when the barman came out to clear my table. I wondered if he had been watching me. He asked me if I would like another beer.

Without hesitation, I said yes please. The barman kindly brought it out to me. I took a sip of my beer, closed my eyes and slouched back on my chair. I was in my element. Warm sun on the face, cool beer in the hand, peace and quiet. Perfect.

Kuwait seemed like a dream, but at the same time terribly real. Did I really do all that? Did I really enter and go through Saudi illegally? My scalp chilled and I shuddered slightly as the enormity of the risk I had taken hit me. Generally though, I was feeling good. It was only my second day in Amsterdam but I was already feeling safe. I enjoyed the sun and the tranquillity for at least an hour before telling myself that all good things had to come to an end. Time I was making tracks, I said to myself. I literally retraced my steps along the canal to get myself back to the tram route.

I had little difficulty in finding a tram stop. I was the only person there. I had been waiting just a minute or so when a tram arrived and stopped to let me on. As soon as I stepped aboard it set off.

I had been expecting to pay the driver, but this clearly wasn't the system. I reasoned that an inspector would come aboard at some point during my journey. Within about five minutes the tram was in the familiar area of the harbour. So, the first time it stopped, without hesitation I jumped off. It was only when the tram was pulling away that I realised I hadn't paid a fare.

Joanna was already in the *John* by the time I got there. 'Hi, darling', I said.' Been waiting long?'

'No, not really,' Joanna replied. 'Less than half an hour.'

'How did the shopping go?'

'Not too bad. Got most things. Oh, by the way, I bought you a shirt. I hope you like it.'

'I will.'

'How about you? See anything interesting on your sight-seeing tour?'

'No, not really. Nothing worth mentioning. But, I discovered that Amsterdam really is a progressive city. Public transport is free. Well, the trams, that is.'

'The trams aren't free. What makes you think they are?'

'Well I've just been on one, and I didn't have to pay a fare. The driver was enclosed in his cab, and there wasn't a conductor on board.'

'The conductor is a machine with a slot into which you put your fare. Or, into which you are *supposed* to put your fare.'

'Oh no, I didn't see it. I feel terrible. Oh well, I'll pay double next time.'

It wasn't long before the subject of food came up. I said I could eat a horse. Joanna said she could too, but just a small one. So, the next time the barman came over to clear our glasses away, I asked him if the bar did food. With a mischievous half-smile on his face he drew my attention to a double door in the back wall of the bar and stated that it gave access to, as the name above it suggested, a restaurant. I looked at Joanna, she looked at me and, without uttering a word we said,

'Let's go.'

We returned to the bar for a last drink, then rolled back to our hotel about eleven.

Life in Amsterdam became an ongoing problem of how to get through each day. Every new day simply presented us with another span of time to kill. In the daytime we went for walks, sat on benches watching the world go by and popped in and out of pubs and cafes. Every evening was a pub-crawl. The problem was my indecisiveness. Had I been able to decide that we were going to have to stay in Amsterdam for three or six months we could've taken steps to improve things. We could each get a job, make new friends, start getting ourselves out to the cinema, theatre and concerts, but I found I couldn't make up my mind as to how long a stay would be necessary.

Joanna kept saying that the decision as to how long we would have to remain in Amsterdam had to be mine, and that we could only return home when I felt it was safe to do so. I knew that Joanna wasn't happy in Amsterdam and that she didn't want to stay there a day longer than was necessary. I kept hoping that I would wake up one morning with a gut feeling that the time was right, that my pursuers had concluded that their having people at Heathrow was now pointless, and that it was safe for me to enter the UK.

As usual, Joanna and I were the only residents who had come down to the dining room for breakfast. However, just as Nella, the breakfast chef-cum-chambermaid was serving our boiled egg and slice of cold ham, two couples came in. Somehow I knew right away they were Americans. While they were settling in at a table there was quite an interactive buzz as we all said good morning. Somebody stated they were from Dallas, Texas. Within a minute Nella came over and placed two breakfasts on the Americans' table. Meantime, I was keeping an anticipatory half-eye on them. Nella came over with another two breakfasts. There was an immediate silence. They're stunned, I said to myself. Soon mutterings started. And, in no time, these had become loud criticisms. Nella was called over and was given an earful of bad-tempered complaints about the skimpiness of the breakfast. I felt sorry for Nella. But I need not have. She remained quite cool. She explained to the Americans that she had no say in the breakfast menu, and added that she would pass on their complaints to the manager. When Joanna and I stood up to leave we turned to the Americans and wished them a nice day. While we were leaving, murmurings of discontent were still rumbling on. I wondered whether we would see the Americans again. On our way upstairs, and in our room, Joanna and I chuckled about what had just happened in the dining room. 'I'm going to have to get some reading material,' I said. 'Fancy a walk round the bookshops?'

'No, you go on by yourself, darling,' replied Joanna. 'I've got a letter to write. And I really must get it away today.'

'I'll leave you to it then,' I said. 'See you later in the *John*. About four?'

'Yes, see you then. Take care, darling,' she added.

I didn't go directly to the shops. I bought an English newspaper and headed for the harbour. I found a bench and settled down to catch up on news from home. I browsed through the first few pages of the paper, paying little attention to their contents. But this immediately changed at the foreign news section. The word 'Kuwait' virtually leapt off the page at me. The article was essentially about the 'near certainty', as the reporter put it, that the Americans had been planning to bump off Saddam Hussein and that, to this end, a small special unit had been preparing and training at a secret location in Kuwait. The Americans have always firmly denied this of course, the article said. But, it went on, Washington was now dropping strong hints that if there ever had been an assassination plot, this had now been dropped. The writer of the article stated that sources were suggesting that most Americans were now thinking along disarmament lines. And, the rest of the article listed several suggestions as to how this could be achieved. I was of course delighted to read that the Americans were now looking at possible new ways of dealing with the perceived threat from Iraq. But I was not jumping up and down on my seat with joy. I immediately began to wonder what the Americans would do with the people who were directly involved in the assassination plan and those who, like me, knew about it. In an attempt to get my mind off my new concerns I pestered my two brain cells with crossword clues for half an hour. They didn't do very well. So, I set off in search of a pub lunch. Eventually, I got myself going in the direction of the city centre and its bookshops.

I had scanned the entire selection of novels offered by one shop and had bought two books, but this whetted my appetite. I wanted more. I had gone into a second shop and was browsing through its crime titles when something made me turn and look out through the shop's front door. There was a restaurant directly opposite and immediately outside it there were two people, chatting and laughing. One was a tall man with blonde wavy hair, the other was Joanna. I slipped deeper into the bookshop and watched. Joanna and the man eventually shook hands and parted. I hesitated for a few minutes, then left the bookshop and headed for the *John.*

In the *John,* I sat at what had become 'our' table. My mind was in a mess. On the way from the bookshop I had considered the possibility that the blonde stranger was a CIA man. Thankfully, I soon saw what a crazy notion that was. Who could he be? A new bit on the side? My God, we've only been here a week. No. No way. Joanna's too honest a person to two-time anybody. Who is he then? Of course, it's simple, he's nobody. She only met him today. She was sitting having lunch alone, he was too, he asked if he could join her, she said why not. They leave the restaurant and, outside, it's a case of 'it was nice meeting you' 'Goodbye.' She'll probably never see him again. She'll tell me all about it when she comes in. Joanna came in with a big smile on her face. 'Nice day?' I asked, as she sat in close to me.

'Not bad,' she answered, still smiling.

'Get your letter written?'
'Er, yes I did. I was glad to get that off.'
'Anything else?'
'Well I got that bag of washing to the laundrette. I was glad to get that done.'
'What about lunch? Did you have a bit of lunch?'
'Yes, a nice little restaurant. Not far from here. We must go there together some time. And what about you? Did you get any books?'
'Yes,' I said, 'a couple.'

During dinner, and later that evening, I don't think I was very good company. And, I doubt whether the single malt I had for the road did anything other than make me, if it were at all possible, even more of a bore.
Next morning, while I was helping Joanna make the bed, I asked her what her plans for the day were.
'I've got quite a busy day,' she replied. 'I'll # probably spend most of the forenoon ironing. Very exciting. But I'm looking forward to the rest of the day. I'm having lunch with Nella. And after that she's going to take me to some of her favourite shops.'
'That's a point,' I said. 'Where do you get ironing done?'
'I do it myself,' Joanna replied with a smile.
'Nella lends me her iron and her ironing board.'
'You're a marvel,' I said.

After a brisk fresh-air-and-exercise walk along the harbour's edge, I set off on my now daily meander through the city's back streets and alleyways. I discovered a new canal and followed it until I found a pub. Then, sustained by beer and sandwiches, I spent most of the middle part of the day sitting outside immersed in one of the who-dunnits I had bought the day before.

I decided that, before going to the *John*, I would pop into the hotel and dump my book. I was within just a few yards of the hotel when the front door opened. It was the blonde man. I went into slow motion. He walked past me. I don't think he looked at me. What could he have been doing in the hotel? He must have been seeing Joanna. I felt like taking a run and a jump into the harbour. Without having abandoned that idea entirely, I carried on into the hotel, and went upstairs. Joanna wasn't in our room or in the bathroom. I was now feeling quite ill and close to tears. I sat on the edge of the bed and tried to pull myself together. I had made an instant assumption as to why the blonde guy had been in the hotel, and, typical of me, I had assumed the worst. At a time like this you are supposed to remain calm, think rationally and consider all the possibilities. Blondie didn't work in the hotel, there's only Vincent and Nella. And I'm sure he's not a resident, unless of course he booked in yesterday.

He bumps into Joanna, they get chatting, he mentions the fact that it's near mid-day and asks Joanna if she would like to join him for lunch, and she says that would be nice, and Joanna hasn't mentioned this simply because it was no big deal.

I decided to pop down to reception to ask Vincent if he had seen Joanna. As soon as I stepped into the foyer, Vincent told me that Joanna was in the dining room. I wondered why he hadn't told me that when I came into the hotel. I asked Vincent who the blonde guy was. He said he didn't know. He said he had only caught a glimpse of him as he was leaving. He said he hadn't seen him come in. Something told me that Vincent was being economical with the truth. I also felt that quizzing him any further would be futile. I merely popped my head round the dining room door. Joanna and Nella were sitting together. I said hello to both and checked with Joanna that I would see her later.

I went back upstairs, showered, changed, and went out.

It was busy outside the hotel. It seemed to be the start of the return of the commuters. I crossed the road and slouched against the canal railings to watch the bustle. People were streaming out of the station, many of them were picking up their bikes and presumably heading home. As ever, it seemed, scores of young backpackers were milling around outside the tourist information centre.

For some reason I had always enjoyed watching people coming and going.

It was only after I had been in the *John* for about ten minutes that I started to wonder why I hadn't popped back into the hotel to wait for Joanna. I certainly didn't want any more time to think on my own. I'd done enough thinking. Blondie's arrival on the scene had compelled me to imagine life without Joanna, and I didn't like what I saw.

Joanna came in just at the point at which I was starting to become anxious as to why she was slightly late. She smiled as she came towards me. This never failed to take my breath away.

'Hi, honey,' she said, brightly.

'Hello,' I said. 'Good day?'

'Not bad.'

Wilhelm, the barman, brought our usual drinks across to our table. He invariably did this now when the bar was quiet.

'How did your lunch and shopping go? I asked.

'Oh, brilliantly, Nella's a delightful person. Great fun to be with. But what about you? What did you do today?'

'Oh, I just went for my now usual wander, sat in the sun, read my book. By the way, I discovered a maritime museum about a mile down the river. I didn't go in. I wondered whether you and I might pop down there tomorrow.'

'Mm, I'll be too busy tomorrow,' replied Joanna.

‘Busy?’

‘Yes, nothing major, just bits and pieces, you know.’

I didn’t know, but I didn’t feel inclined to ask. At that point I found myself sinking into myself. I became moody, perversely wallowing in self-pity.

That entire evening must have been a dreadful experience for Joanna. I must have been about as entertaining as a Zombie who had lost the will to live. I was well aware of this but could do nothing about it. There was no way I could have been amusing and interesting. I had been in this sort of situation before. I wondered why when I suspected my partner was thinking about leaving me, I invariably behaved in such a way as to convince her that she was making the right decision. Why *does* Joanna stick with me?

Next morning, on our way back upstairs after breakfast, I asked Joanna again if she fancied a visit to the maritime museum. She apologised again and said she had too many things to do. She told me to carry on by myself, and said she would see me later. I bought an English newspaper and set off along the footpath by the river. It was outrageously early for a drink but for some reason I found myself almost automatically turning into the first pub I came to. I settled into a window table, took a sip of my beer and unfolded my paper. As I scanned the main headlines, I quite unintentionally caught sight of the day's date. It was my birthday. Surprise, surprise, I said to myself. I didn't know whether to be happy or sad. I told myself to be happy. I thought about having a second beer to celebrate my birthday, but I decided not to. I was keen to get on with my visit to the museum.

I thoroughly enjoyed my browse through the museum building and probably enjoyed even more my exploration of the replica wooden galleon that was tied up there. I must get Joanna along here sometime, I said to myself.

Rather than go directly back to the hotel I decided to make a detour via what I had sussed was the area known as Old Amsterdam. As a lover of all things quaint I knew that if there were examples of very old buildings it would be a place I would enjoy exploring. When I came to an alleyway that was little more than six feet wide, I reasoned that this would be a street that would contain the sort of houses I would find interesting. The houses were certainly interesting, but not, from my point view, for the right sort of reason. I was in another red underwear district. I strode smartly through the area, but knowing there were near-naked women on display, I found it impossible to refrain from occasionally glancing to the left and to the right. The old city did indeed contain many very old and interesting buildings and I was glad I decided to check it out.

A very modern-looking pub in the area stuck out like the proverbial sore thumb. And, I think this as much as anything encouraged me to pop in for a quick one.

When I got to the bar I looked and looked again at the barmaid. She was topless. I had always assumed that these sort of attractions were restricted to late evening, so I found mind-boggling my being served in the early afternoon by a half-naked woman. I had intended to have just one drink, but when I placed my empty glass onto the bar I found myself ordering a second.

By the time I got back to the hotel it was mid-afternoon. I asked Vincent if Joanna was in. He simply said no. I went on up, showered and changed. Having no idea as to where Joanna might be, I decided to go straight to the *John* and wait for her there.

Entering the *John* somehow reminded me that it was my birthday, and I considered celebrating with a sneaky, early single malt. However, with the miserable evening I had subjected Joanna to the night before in mind, I was clear that there was absolutely no way I could risk ending up a gibbering pain-in-the-ass tonight. Celebrating my birthday was the least of my concerns. I somehow had to redeem myself. Perhaps dinner at a posh restaurant would be a good start. As the clock above the bar and my watch crept on and on beyond four, I switched from thumb-twiddling to nail-biting.

Calm down, I said to myself, there's probably a simple reason why she is late. But I found staying calm difficult. As the minutes ticked past, my fears grew. At a quarter to five I started to think there was something wrong, by five o clock I knew there was. I tried to decide what to do. I didn't want to overreact, but I felt I had to do something. Just at that the phone behind the bar rang. I seemed to know it was Joanna. Wilhelm answered it. As he put the phone down he turned to me and said,

'Can you go back to your hotel, please, Jack?' I thanked Wilhelm for taking the call and immediately left the bar.

As I walked smartly back to the hotel my thoughts were entirely negative. I had a lump in my throat and butterflies in my stomach. Tears filled my eyes but I managed to not let them flow. I didn't want Joanna to see I had been upset. I could not think of any good reason as to why Joanna would leave me waiting for an hour, then call me back to the hotel. This is it, I said to myself. We're not going out tonight. It's over.

As soon as I entered the hotel Vincent told me that Joanna was in the dining room. I opened the dining room door. The room was in darkness save for the soft glow surrounding a cluster of small lighted candles. The light from the tiny flames was just bright enough to betray the presence of several people. Suddenly, in little more than a whisper voices began to sing *Happy Birthday*. I stared and listened in near disbelief. Those moments were probably the most moving I had ever experienced. Just a few minutes before, thinking that my world was falling apart, I felt I was close to breaking down. Again, I was close to tears, but now for wonderfully different reasons. Everything before me was telling me that all was well between Joanna and me. I was a hugely relieved and very happy man. When the singing stopped the light came on. In the room were Joanna, Nella, the Americans, two Japanese couples and a young man with long hair. Everybody applauded and cheered. Joanna threw her arms round me and hugged me tightly.

'Happy birthday, darling,' she whispered.

The popping of a champagne cork elicited more cheers. Nella pushed a glass of bubbles into my hand. As if from nowhere, a waitress appeared with a trolley and covered two tables with all sorts of food. There was a variety of drinks on a separate table. The birthday cake was huge and beautifully decorated. My blowing out the candles drew another round of cheers. Nella asked everybody to help themselves to food and drink. Music started playing from somewhere and this sparked off what developed into a happy party atmosphere in which everybody danced, sang, laughed and chatted.

I danced with Nella. I discovered that she was a student and that she would be resuming her studies in the autumn. She mentioned that the young man with the long hair was a fellow student. I asked her if he was her boyfriend. After laughing, she rather coyly admitted that he was. When I half-jokingly asked her about marriage, her mood changed and she quite sternly stated that no way would she ever get married. For some reason this saddened me slightly.

At one point, while I was chatting with a Japanese man, something made me look to my right. My heart sank. It was Blondie. He was talking to Joanna. On seeing me glancing across, Joanna called me over. She introduced Blondie as Nicki and told me that he was the owner of *Nicki's,* the restaurant she had mentioned to me the day before. She added that Nicki had done the catering for the evening, and that he had got his head chef to bake the cake. She said that she had got to know Nicki quite well as a result of frequent visits to his restaurant during previous visits to Amsterdam. All at the same time I felt happy, relieved, and silly. The last I remember of the evening was Joanna pouring me a large measure of my favourite single malt.

We didn't make it to breakfast next morning. We eventually dragged ourselves out of bed shortly before midday. Joanna suggested our grabbing a coffee somewhere and going for a stroll by the river. I agreed enthusiastically. While we strolled, right out of the blue Joanna asked me about my childhood. 'Why do you ask?' I said.

'Oh, I simply find people's formative years interesting. I like to know what a person was like as a child.'

I found myself admitting to Joanna that I didn't have an entirely happy childhood. She asked if there was a particular reason for this. I told Joanna that as a very small boy I saw life as being very unfair. I explained that this was largely because any time something got broken while my sister and I were skylarking she insisted that I was the guilty one. And, my father always believed her. I said I didn't mind getting the slipper, it was the unfairness of it all that got to me. 'Right up to my early teens my dad blamed me for just about everything that somehow got broken or damaged,' I said. 'He accused me of breaking flowers in the garden, making stains and dirty marks on carpets and walls, everything. He even tried to get me to admit to having fiddled with his hi-fi when it went on the blink. I came to believe that my sister was deliberately damaging things knowing that I would be blamed and punished.'

'How do you get on with your father and your sister now?'

'Oh, wonderfully well,' I replied, I dearly love them both'

'No hard feelings at all?' Joanna asked.

'No. My sister was simply my dad's pet. I

don't blame him for that. It's very common. And my sister's behaviour was simply sibling rivalry. That too is very normal.'

I asked Joanna about her childhood.

'Another day' she replied.

We walked on in silence for a while. All of a sudden I found myself asking Joanna if she would like to fly home tomorrow.

'It's still early,' she said. ' Why wait till tomorrow?'

'You're right.'

Chapter Twelve

During the flight from Amsterdam we agreed our first moves on arriving at Heathrow. Get to Chiswick, book into a small hotel, pop into an accommodation bureau in the morning and search for a small flat.

In London, everything went to plan. We ended up in a bed-sitter though, rather than in a flat. But, it was large and beautifully decorated. On our first afternoon we went shopping to stock up the fridge. As it neared teatime Joanna decided she would have to have a bath and wash her hair, so I had to volunteer to do the cooking.

Joanna had started a discussion about accommodation the day before but it was only now, as I waited for the rice to boil, that the full significance of today's events dropped into my mind. Joanna and I were living together.

Later that evening we went to our local phone-box to ring our folks. We went into the kiosk separately. Joanna went in first. When I got in, it was my mother that answered. She told me that there was a letter for me. I asked her to open it and read the gist of it to me over the phone. It was from George. He apologized for his having done a runner without telling me but explained that he hadn't told a soul, not even Liz, in case the College got wind of his plans. He was working in Toulouse and said he would keep in touch through my parents. I said hello to my dad and asked him to give my love to my sister. On leaving the box Joanna said, 'Well?'

'Oh,' I said, 'they're fine. How about your lot?'

'Yes, they're fine too.'

On the way back to the house I said little. I couldn't think clearly. In our room, Joanna stopped me as I went to switch on the telly. 'Something's troubling you, darling,' she said. 'Lets talk. Maybe I can help.'

'I'm just very confused,' I said.

Joanna said, 'I'm not entirely surprised. It's easy to say, I know, but it is true, time will heal. You've been through a lot. For several weeks you have been in a state of fear. But nobody is after you now. You're safe. Soon it will all be behind you. Please try to be patient. Try to relax.'

'Did you think I was losing my marbles out there?'

'No, I did not. For all I knew the College could well have been a front for something. You had sussed things and knew things that I didn't know.'

'But the boarded-up room on the third floor, you knew about that, I said. Weren't you suspicious? Didn't you ever wonder what was being hidden in there?'

'I knew exactly what was in there. I used to work in that room. I used to help churn out the College's prospectus, newsletters and various hand bills.'

'You knew? Why didn't you tell me?'

'I had virtually sworn an oath of absolute secrecy about the print room. During the invasion the Iraqis discovered computers and printers in the American School and smashed them up. On hearing about this, the English School and the College immediately took steps to conceal our equipment. This was successful. After the war the English School opened up their print room, and started producing their little prospectus and newsletter again. However, some terrorist cell in Kuwait, apparently regarding this literature as western propaganda, promptly broke into the school and smashed everything up. Purely by chance we hadn't got round to opening up our print room, and, of course, on hearing this news we left things as they were. David asked the staff at that time to be totally tight-lipped about the print room. He said that even if the terrorists just heard about it, they would probably decide to destroy it. Not that long ago somebody broke into the print room. Mysteriously though, they didn't touch the equipment. But we couldn't go to the police in case news about our having such a facility got out.'

'Okay, that explains the existence of the secret room, but what about the passports, I asked? You can't tell me that the College's taking and holding on to our passports wasn't simply a way of stopping us leaving Kuwait.'

'Jack, if you had gone to David and told him you were packing in your job and that you wanted your passport back, he would have given it to you. The two blokes that disappeared before you and George arrived demanded their passports, and even though David suspected that they were planning doing a runner, he gave them back their passports. It's the immigration people. They give the College practically no notice at all when they want residency applications submitted. They simply phone and say they are now ready to process the next batch. They then expect these to be at their office almost within the hour. This is why David has to have all the passports to hand at all times.'

'But wasn't the disappearance of those two blokes a mystery?'

'No, they went back to the UK. Liz heard from one of them and Margaret received a letter from the other.'

'Why do so many people do a runner?'

'It's the contract. They don't want to pay the penalties for breach.'

'I'd forgotten about that. Well, if there was nothing sinister going on out there, why was somebody spying on us?'

'Who was spying?'

'No matter what number we dialled for a taxi it was always Anwar that turned up. Our telephone must have been being tapped. Anwar must have been a spy.'

'No, it was just that Anwar was probably the taxi man for the Dasmah area. Arabs rarely compete with each other. They're not competitive people. They prefer to co-operate with each other. So, when you phone a Hawalli or a Salyma number, for example, that office would simply contact Anwar to tell him he had a pick-up in his area.'

I was starting to think that I had been entirely wrong about everything, and that I had been acting like a complete idiot, when I suddenly remembered the fax in David's office. 'Well,' I said, 'I still think there was something dodgy going on at the College. I saw a fax in David's office. It was about George and me. It said we seemed to be ideal because we had little contact with the UK and that we had agreed to do the Arabic classes. What was all that about?'

'That was largely to do with the problem of so many people not completing their contract. It was felt that tied people with families were the ones that would have most difficulty settling in Kuwait. So, David asked the recruitment agency in the UK to slightly discriminate in favour of single men without close family connections. It didn't really work. As for the language classes, they were set up largely as a result of staff demand. Many of the teachers felt that a good knowledge of the local language and culture would help them to settle into the Kuwait community.'

'But the fax was addressed to number one. That sounds a bit secretive to me,' I said. Joanna laughed. 'That's Hassan. He's the owner of the College. I've met him several times. He's a lovely man. He lives in Cairo. David always refers to him as number one.'

That's it, I said to myself, there's no doubt now. I'd been wrong, about everything. What a pillock. How could I have been such an absolute idiot? I went into my bag and dug out my duty-free bottle of single malt. I asked Joanna if she would join me.

'I'd love to,' she replied. 'But let's just have small ones. We don't want to get all sleepy, do we?'

'Small ones it is,' I said.

Joanna never did say anything about whether she would ever want to go back to Kuwait, and I never asked. Within a month of our arriving in London we each had found a new job. And this enabled us to rent a super flat in the Bedford Park area of Chiswick. And, we were happy. Things could hardly have been better. And then it happened.

We were strolling along the high road in Chiswick one Saturday morning, looking in shop windows, popping in and out of places, gradually working our way along to the supermarket. From a passing cab somebody waved. I peered towards the car. It was Anwar.

'Look who that is,' I said.
'Who is it?' asked Joanna.
'Its Anwar.'
'That's not Anwar.'
'Yes it is,' I insisted. 'Add Arab clothes'
'No it isn't,' Joanna said again, this time quite angrily.

I decided not to argue. In next to no time the incident was over, and the car had gone. Joanna and I agreed to disagree about whether or not it was Anwar that was in that taxi. But that was not the end of the matter. I could not stop thinking about what Anwar was doing in Chiswick. Was it just a huge co-incidence? Was he on holiday? Had I described Chiswick in glowing terms to him one day? Will he look me up? I decided to try to put the incident out of my mind for the time being. Although, I felt certain that his being in Chiswick had to have something to do with me. I would probably answer the door of the flat some evening and a couple of heavies would barge their way in. I'd be bound and gagged and shoved into the back of a car. Possibly drugged. Maybe I would wake up in Kuwait, if I ever woke up at all.

Days later, I still hadn't rid myself of my concerns about Anwar's appearance in Chiswick. I kept these worries from Joanna but I felt sure she sussed that I wasn't an entirely happy man. She started talking about the possibility of our moving out of London.

Perhaps down to my hometown of Penzance. She didn't say so but I was certain that her thoughts about moving were related to her being sure that I was still agonising over having seen Anwar in Chiswick.

Before long, we did relocate to Cornwall. We got new jobs there and took out a mortgage. At that point, I realised I had become semi-detached suburban Mr. Average. My memory of Kuwait gradually faded. Eventually it all seemed like a vivid dream. On the one or two occasions that Chiswick was mentioned, Joanna repeated her insistence that it wasn't Anwar that was in that taxi. But, if it wasn't Anwar, who was it? No, that definitely was Anwar. But then, maybe it wasn't.